water
sapphire

water
sapphire

Belinda Ray

SCHOLASTIC INC.
New York Toronto London Auckland Sydney
Mexico City New Delhi Hong Kong Buenos Aires

For my father who, with his whistling and singing,
provided the musical soundtrack to my childhood.

ISBN 0-439-77515-9

Copyright © 2005 by Alloy Entertainment
All rights reserved.
Published by Scholastic Inc.

ALLOYENTERTAINMENT   Produced by Alloy Entertainment
151 West 26th Street, New York, NY 10001

12 11 10 9 8 7 6 5 4 3 2 1   5 6 7 8 9 10/0

Printed in the U.S.A.   40
First printing, December 2005

CHAPTER
One

"It's hopeless," Amanda Littlefield said as she examined the list on Mr. Hupp's classroom door. "I should just drop out."

The list, which Mr. Hupp had posted just moments earlier, contained the names of five sixth graders who were running for the student council seat about to be vacated by Madeleine Heimburg. Maddie was transferring schools in the spring, and Amanda had been hoping she could fill Maddie's seat, but after seeing the other names on the list, she wasn't so sure. She turned her discouraged gaze to her two best friends, Keisha Johnson and Sam Sullivan, who were standing behind her.

"No way, Amanda," Sam said. "You can't drop out."

"Yeah, you'd be a great student council rep," Keisha added.

Amanda liked to think that was true. She really wanted to make school a better place for students. After all, weren't students what a school was all about? It was so easy for the grown-ups to just take over and decide that they knew how everything should be done, but she really believed the students should have a voice. She wanted to create a student lounge where kids could hang out during study halls. She wanted to start a school-wide recycling program. She wanted to do lots of things, and getting them done would be a lot easier if she were on the student council. But she needed to be elected first.

If only she'd known at the beginning of the school year that the student council was more than just a bunch of kids sitting around in the auditorium eating pretzels every Thursday afternoon at three o'clock, she would have run for office then. Unfortunately, the current members of the student council didn't use their positions to do anything but plan dances, but Amanda intended to change that. If she was elected.

"We need someone like you on the student council," Keisha added.

"Yeah, someone pushy," Sam joked.

Amanda gave her friends a half smile. She appreciated their support, but the writing was on the wall—or rather, on Mr. Hupp's door. "Face it, you guys, I don't stand a chance."

"Sure, you do," Keisha said. She smoothed back her unruly dark hair with one hand as she spoke. It was long enough to pull back into a ponytail now, but little curls were always springing loose here and there and driving Keisha crazy. "You can beat Jesse Hunter and Tracy Meyers."

"Maybe," Amanda said, glancing back at the list on their math teacher's door, "but they're not the ones I'm worried about."

Keisha sighed. "Okay, so Jenna Scott will probably get a lot of votes," she admitted. Jenna Scott was the most popular girl in the sixth grade—possibly even in the whole school. "But not *everyone* is going to vote for her."

"No, the rest of them will be voting for Noah Carpenter," Amanda said.

"*What?*" Keisha exclaimed. She leaned forward and gazed at the list over Amanda's shoulder. "Ohmigosh. Noah's running, too?"

Noah Carpenter was nearly as popular as Jenna Scott. He was the only sixth grader who had a starting position on the soccer team, and he'd been named Most Valuable Player at the sports banquet last month. He was pretty tall for his age, about five-nine, so people were already expecting him to get a key position on the basketball team, too. All the boys respected him for being such a super athlete. And with his dark curly hair, deep brown eyes, and darkly tanned skin, all the sixth-grade girls—and even some of the older ones—thought he was really cute.

Amanda nodded. "Mm-hm. Mr. *and* Ms. Popularity are in the race. Which is why I don't stand a chance."

Keisha wrinkled her nose at Amanda's comment, but she didn't disagree. Sam, on the other hand, was rolling his eyes.

"Come on," he said. "You can't give up just because a couple of popular kids are running against you. You're much smarter than Noah and Jenna. When it's time for speeches, you'll blow them away."

Amanda cocked her head and stared at her friend. Sam might be right about that. All of the candidates for the student council seat had to give speeches on the day of the election to tell everyone what they planned to do if they won, and Amanda knew she could probably give a better speech than either Noah or Jenna; she'd always been good at oral reports. But something told her that being a good speaker wasn't going to be enough.

"I don't know, Sam," she said. "This is middle school. Popularity is everything, unfortunately. People aren't going to vote for me just because of my student lounge idea."

"I am," Keisha said. "And you will, won't you?"

"That makes two votes, Keisha," Amanda said. "Not enough to win an election." She turned to Sam. "Too bad you're in the seventh grade. If you were a year younger, I might get three."

"You'll get more than three votes," Sam said.

"Okay, maybe four," Amanda said. "Five, tops. Either way, I'm not going to beat both Jenna *and* Noah, so I might as well drop out now and save myself the embarrassment." Amanda started toward Mr. Hupp's room, but Sam grabbed her by the elbow.

"Wait a second," he said. "Aren't you forgetting something?" He lifted Amanda's hand and pinched the bracelet on her wrist between his thumb and forefinger.

Amanda glanced down at the charm bracelet that Keisha had given to her. "No, I'm not forgetting anything," she said, shaking her arm free. How could she? The bracelet had worked magic for Keisha—Amanda and Sam had seen it with their own eyes! And Amanda hadn't taken off the bracelet since Keisha had clasped it on her wrist yesterday after school—not for swim practice, not for bed, not to shower, not for anything. Just knowing that she had the bracelet and feeling the weight of its chain and its swinging charms gave her confidence a boost. But still, just because the magic worked for Keisha, didn't mean it would work for her.

"I'm just not sure it could help," she told her friends.

Sam's eyes nearly doubled in size. "Are you kidding? It's *magic*, Amanda."

"Well, who knows if it will work a second time?" Amanda replied. "Besides, unless it can somehow make both Jenna and Noah drop out of the race, I don't think it's going to help."

"So . . . what? You're just going to give up?" Sam asked. "Quit without even trying?" His blue eyes, which were normally placid, suddenly seemed fiery.

Amanda scrunched her eyebrows together. "Since when do you care whether or not I run for student council?"

"Since you *stopped* caring," Sam replied. "The Amanda Littlefield I know wouldn't back away from a challenge."

"This isn't a challenge, Sam. This is a defeat before it's begun," Amanda said. She looked to Keisha for support, but Keisha just shrugged.

"You did say you didn't want a bunch of gingerbreads running the school," she said.

Gingerbreads was the term Amanda used to refer to all the students who dressed alike, talked alike, listened to the same music, and had all the same opinions. It was short for *gingerbread people*—people who seemed like they'd all been shaped with the same cookie cutter.

Amanda stared down at her feet, kicking at a crack in the floor tile with the toe of her red Converse sneaker. It was true. She didn't want to see either Noah or Jenna—the king and queen of the gingerbreads—elected to the student council. Neither one of them would try to make positive changes in the school. They'd just plan more dances. But how was Amanda supposed to win against them? And what was the point of trying?

"It's not that I want them to—" Amanda started, but she didn't get to finish.

"See, Noah?" Jenna Scott suddenly said, sauntering in front of Amanda and pointing at the list on Mr. Hupp's door. "I told you you're my only competition."

Jenna pulled Noah closer to the door with her free arm. While he read the names on the list, she smirked over her shoulder at her two lackeys, Sarah Robbins and Emily Reisman. Sarah and Emily had once been Keisha's two best friends, but they'd abandoned Keisha when Jenna started inviting them to hang out with her instead. The prospect of being part of the popular crowd had obviously meant more to them than Keisha's friendship.

"It's totally between the two of you," Emily said with a smug smile.

"Yeah, no one else on that list has got a chance," Sarah added, and the two of them giggled.

Out of the corner of her eye, Amanda saw Keisha gaping. On her other side, Sam was standing with his arms folded across his chest and a big scowl on his face. At first, Amanda assumed the scowl was for Jenna and her annoying friends, but then it occurred to her that Sam might actually be scowling at *her* for wanting to give up the race without a fight.

"In a way, I'm kind of glad you're running," Jenna told Noah, twirling her long dark hair in her left hand. "If you weren't, the election would be totally boring."

Amanda groaned. She was beginning to feel like she deserved Sam's scowl, whether it was meant for her or not. How could she look herself in the eye if she didn't at least *try* to beat Jenna? Amanda took a step forward, removing her hands from the large square pockets on the front of her red-and-black-plaid miniskirt and placing them on her hips. "You have more competition than just Noah, you know," she said.

She felt Sam beaming beside her as she spoke. Jenna, on the other hand, turned around and frowned at Amanda as if she were an annoying piece of lint on a new sweater.

"What?" Jenna asked. "You?" Then she laughed. "Did you hear that, Noah? Amanda's running for student council, too. Aren't you scared?" She tugged on Noah's sleeve to get his attention, but he ignored her. He was staring at Keisha with a strange expression.

"Friday night was really cool," he said, referring to the multicultural dance that

Keisha, Sam, and Amanda had helped decorate. "I took home one of the flags—a white one with two blue stripes and a sort of sun thing in the middle."

Amanda rolled her eyes. *That's Argentina's flag, you dork,* she thought.

"You mean Argentina?" Keisha asked, her dark eyes wide.

Oh, please, Amanda thought. Did Keisha have to act so fascinated by every syllable Noah spoke?

"Yeah, I think so," Noah replied.

Keisha's face lit up. "I made that one," she said.

"I figured. You said you did most of the flags. Anyway, it's really cool. I have it hanging in my room."

Amanda looked on as Keisha grinned and then blinked away bashfully. It was almost painful to watch. "Sorry to interrupt," she said, unable to stomach any more of her friend's crush-inspired behavior, "but we have to get to homeroom."

"So do we," Jenna said, grabbing Noah's arm possessively. "Come on, Noah."

"See ya," Noah said, nodding his head to

Keisha as he walked away. Keisha nodded back, but she didn't say anything.

"Oh, by the way, Amanda," Jenna called back over her shoulder, "good luck! You're going to need it."

As Jenna and Noah disappeared around the corner, Sam thrust his fist into the air. "Yea, Amanda!" he cheered. "I knew you couldn't back down from a fight."

Amanda sighed heavily. "Too bad I can't win it."

"Would you stop with that?" Sam said. He ran a hand through his bushy brown hair, making it stand up even more than it already did.

"It's true, Sam," Amanda said. "Just ask Keisha. She knows. She's probably going to vote for Noah."

Keisha turned at the mention of her name. "What are you kidding? I'm voting for you, Amanda."

"Really?" Amanda asked. "Even if Noah asks you out or something?"

Keisha screwed up her face. "He's not going to ask me out. And even if he did, what makes you think I'd say yes?"

"*You took my Argentina flag home*?" Sam

mimicked, pressing his hands over the front pocket of his red velour shirt. "*How romantic.*"

"Sam!" Keisha protested. "I didn't say that!"

Amanda giggled at Sam's imitation. "It was pretty close."

Keisha crossed her arms. "It was not. But either way, I'm still voting for you."

Amanda smiled at Keisha. She was glad her friend hadn't been completely taken over by her crush.

"Amanda, would you get moving?" Sam said. "You just told Jenna you were going to give her some competition, so let's do it."

"How?"

"I already told you," Sam said, pointing at the bracelet again. "All we need is a plan and a little magic."

"I still don't—"

"Sam's right, Amanda," Keisha interrupted. "You can't just give up. And we should at least give the bracelet a chance."

Amanda took a deep breath and let it out slowly. "I guess," she said, fingering the tiger's-eye charm that Keisha had added to the bracelet.

"Cool. I have to work at my mom's shop after school today," Keisha said. "Why don't you guys meet me there and we'll see what we come up with."

"Sounds good," Sam said.

"Okay," Amanda agreed. Still, she couldn't help being skeptical about her chances. What had Jenna said? *Good luck! You're going to need it*? That was the truth. But Amanda knew it was going to take more than just luck for her to get on the student council. It was going to take a miracle.

CHAPTER
Two

"This is awesome," Sam said, trying on a medieval helmet at Keisha's mother's antique store. He pulled the metal visor down over his face and gave a fierce growl, but Amanda and Keisha just giggled. It was hard to take him seriously with all the tufts of wild brown hair sticking out through the vents.

"I wonder if knights had that problem," Keisha said, pointing to the top of Sam's head.

"Only the ones with hair like Sam's," Amanda replied, though she doubted there could have been many of them. Sam's hair was unique. It was thick, brown, and wavy, and it stood straight out from his head in all directions, refusing to lie down even though it was nearly five inches long. Sometimes he got teased in school because of it, but Sam never seemed to care. That was one of the reasons he and Amanda got along so well—they were both a little offbeat.

Amanda's hair was dark brown, wavy, and long, but she typically wore it wound up into two tight buns on top of her head, because she hated taking the time to dry or style it in the morning. What she really wanted were dreadlocks, but her mother insisted that she comb her hair after every shower, telling her the dreadlocks had to wait until she was older. For now, her mother had said, Amanda would have to settle for expressing her nonconformity through her clothing.

So, instead of wearing cute capri pants and snazzy baby T's like the rest of her class, Amanda paired high black boots with plaid miniskirts and long, belted cardigan sweaters. She wore knee-high argyle socks with chunky-heeled shoes and polyester tops with funky patterns. She accessorized with short scarves tied around her head or neck, dangly earrings, and lots of silver and gemstone rings on her fingers.

Most of her favorite things came from local thrift stores, and she had a great time mixing and matching outfits. It was beyond her how her classmates could be satisfied dressing themselves according to the covers of various teen magazines. For Amanda, the more outrageous the outfit, the more fun it was to wear. It was like celebrating Halloween every day.

Of course, as a result of their atypical looks, neither Amanda nor Sam had ever been particularly popular. On most occasions, Amanda didn't mind. But now that she was running for student council, it had occurred to her that being different might not work in her favor.

Sam lifted the visor, pushed his hair into the helmet and out of the way as best he could, then lowered the visor again and turned to Amanda. "Is that better?" he asked.

"Loads," she replied, giving him two thumbs-up.

Sam growled again, brandishing an umbrella at his friends. Then he turned to Keisha's mother. "Where did you get this, anyway?" he asked, his voice sounding hollow and far away.

"At an estate sale last weekend," Mrs. Johnson replied. "It was in the bottom of a box of old clothes. I had no idea I'd bought it until I got back here and started unpacking things."

"Wow. Great find," Sam said, lifting the helmet off his head. He turned it over in his hands a few times. "This is a clamshell close helmet. It's probably from the fifteenth century or so. I bet you could get a couple of hundred dollars for it."

Mrs. Johnson placed her hand over her heart. "That's amazing, Sam," she said. "That's exactly what the appraiser told me."

"Really?" Sam said, grinning.

"Sam's way into armor and weapons and stuff," Amanda said. "He has been ever since we were, like, six."

"Your knowledge is impressive, Sam," Mrs. Johnson said. "Next time I end up with an item like this, I'll skip the appraiser and call you instead." Sam grinned again, this time showing the braces on his upper teeth and the black and blue bands he had chosen at the orthodontist's office.

"Keisha," Mrs. Johnson turned toward her daughter, "I have to run to the bank. Can you keep an eye on the register?"

"Sure," Keisha replied.

"And if anyone has any questions, I'll be back in ten minutes, okay?"

"No problem," Keisha said.

Amanda looked around. There were only four or five people in the store at the moment, and they all seemed to be looking at the clothing. They probably wouldn't have a lot of questions, which meant that she, Keisha, and Sam might get a chance to get down to business with the bracelet.

Obviously, Keisha had been thinking the same thing, because as soon as Mrs. Johnson was gone, her eyes lit up. "Are you guys ready?" she asked. "Ten minutes should be plenty of time to do what we need to do."

"Let's go," Sam said, his blue eyes flickering with excitement. "Where's the book?"

The book he was referring to was a collection of fairy tales that had, as the three friends found out just recently, once belonged to Amanda's grandmother. A few short months ago, Keisha had found the book in her mom's store on the very same day that her friend from New Hampshire had sent her the charm bracelet, and together the two had worked magic for her.

"In the office," Keisha said. "I left it there when I was working over the weekend." She started toward the front of the store, heading for the door just behind the cash register. Sam was right behind Keisha, and Amanda followed him, trailing her hand along the surfaces of tables and shelves as she walked.

A brass vase with several mermaids etched

on its sides caught her eye and she wondered if the bracelet had the power to bring one of them to life. "Do we have to use the book?" she asked.

Keisha lifted one shoulder in a half shrug. "I don't think so," she said. "I mean, it's the bracelet that's magic, right? Not the book. But I asked Jasmine if she knew how the bracelet worked, and she didn't have a clue, so I thought it would be easier to just go with what we know."

Jasmine was the friend who had given the bracelet to Keisha. She and Keisha had gone to the same elementary school for two years and had become really close. Since then, Jasmine had moved to New Hampshire, but they still kept in touch. And when Keisha was having a rough time at the beginning of the school year, Jasmine had sent her the bracelet for good luck.

"I guess that makes sense," Amanda said.

"Don't worry," Sam told her. "That book is full of pictures. I'm sure we can find someone—or something—to help you with the student council race."

Amanda nodded and tried to think positive, but it was hard to stay optimistic. Short of cheating, which she refused to do, she wasn't sure there was anything that could help her win, magic or otherwise.

Mrs. Johnson's office was immaculate, which didn't surprise Amanda all that much. Even though it was a secondhand shop, Something Old, Something New was incredibly tidy. It was obvious that Keisha's mom had a knack for organization.

Keisha walked to the file cabinet on the back wall and opened the bottom drawer. "This is where Mom puts all of the stuff I leave lying around," she said. "She makes me clean it out once a week." Inside the drawer, Amanda could see a notebook, a box of colored pencils, a baseball, the large blue book of fairy tales, and what looked like a bright gold statue.

"What's *that*?" Amanda asked as Keisha started to reach for the book.

"This?" Keisha removed the statue from the drawer. "It's a woman bowling. It's from an old trophy my mother won a long time ago. She had it in the shop to be sold, but when I was dusting on Saturday it broke. Mom was going to throw it away, but I liked it, so she said I could keep it." Keisha turned the statue around in her hands. "I'm not sure what I'm going to do with it yet."

"Maybe we can bring it to life," Sam suggested.

"Why? So the little gold woman can teach me how to throw strikes?" Amanda asked.

"Yeah, I'm not sure the bowling lady is our best bet," Keisha agreed, putting the statue back in the file cabinet. Then, she withdrew the book of fairy tales and laid it on her mother's desk. She turned to Sam and Amanda. "So how do you want to do this?" she asked.

"Let's just flip through until we see a picture of something that might help," Sam said.

Keisha looked to Amanda. Amanda shrugged. "Might as well." After all, she didn't have a better idea.

"Why don't *you* turn the pages, Amanda?" Keisha suggested. "You're the one we're trying to help."

"Okay," Amanda said. Reaching down, she opened the book's heavy blue cover, admiring the gold lettering, which spelled out *Faerie Tales* in a fancy script. Carefully, she turned the thick, glossy pages, skipping past the table of contents to the first picture.

From the story of Cinderella, it was an illustration of the wicked stepsisters and their mother. "Suddenly, the bowling lady doesn't seem like such a bad idea," Amanda said.

Keisha giggled. "Keep going. Maybe there's a picture of the fairy godmother."

"A little bibbidi-bobbidi-boo could be good," Sam said. Both Amanda and Keisha shot him sideways glances. "What? It's the song she sings," Sam said. "In the movie." Sam scowled. "Just keep flipping," he told Amanda.

Amanda turned back to the book and flipped through the rest of the story. Unfortunately, there were only two other pictures: one of Cinderella dancing with the prince and one of her trying on the glass slipper, but none of the fairy godmother.

"Too bad," Keisha said. "It would have been nice for Sam to meet his idol." Amanda grinned at Sam, who was feigning a smile, and then went back to flipping pages.

The next story was a variation of "The Three Little Pigs," and since Amanda had no use for pigs, big bad wolves, or bundles of hay, sticks, or bricks, she kept going. After that came "Snow White," followed by "Sleeping Beauty," and then "Rumplestiltskin." Amanda was just about to give up hope—how could any of these characters or their stories help her?—when Sam suddenly called out, "Wait!"

"What?" Amanda asked.

"Go back a page," Sam told her. She did as he requested and found herself staring at a beautiful illustration of an ocean surrounded by glaciers and filled with ships with rectangular red-and-white sails.

Amanda squinted at the picture. "Hey, aren't those—?"

"Viking ships," Sam said, his voice full of awe.

Amanda rolled her eyes. "Sam, we're looking for someone to help me win the student council race, not a bunch of thugs to plunder and pillage the school."

"Hey, the Vikings weren't all about plundering and pillaging. They were farmers, too, you know," Sam said. "And, anyway, they're not what I'm looking at." He pointed to the top of the picture, and at first Amanda thought he'd gone crazy.

"What? You want to bring the clouds out of the book?"

"No-o," Sam said. "Her." Again he pointed toward the top of the picture, and this time when Amanda looked, she realized that something else was there. Hidden in the wispy mist, almost obscured by fog and clouds, was a woman's face.

"It's Freyja," Sam said. "The Norse goddess of battle."

Both Amanda and Keisha turned toward their friend. "How do you know all this stuff?" Keisha asked.

"I don't know," Sam said with a shrug. "I just do."

"Well, can she, you know . . . bibbidi-bobbidi-bop?" Keisha asked with a flourish of her arm.

"It's bibbidi-bobbidi-*boo*," Sam said. "But yeah, I think so. I mean, she's a goddess. She should be able to make stuff happen, right?"

"You would think so," Amanda said. "But what's she the goddess of?"

Sam raised his eyebrows, his blue eyes sparkling. "That's the best part," he replied. "She's not just the goddess of battles, she's the goddess of wealth and love, too. Next to Odin—he's the big one, the father of all the gods—Freyja was one of the most powerful beings around. We even have a day of the week named after her."

"We don't have a Freyja-day," Keisha protested.

"No, but we have *Fri*day, and that was Freyja's day. Thursday was Thor's day, for the Norse god of thunder, and Wednesday came from Odin's day."

"Sam, you're a walking encyclopedia," Amanda said.

Sam shrugged. "I like this stuff," he said. "But back to Freyja. She was also the queen of the Valkyries, you know."

"Definition, please," Amanda said.

"They were the female warriors who rode winged horses and carried spears. No one messed with them."

Amanda examined the face in the clouds. The woman she saw there was beautiful. She had long light hair and clear blue eyes, but there was something a bit fierce about her expression. Amanda wondered if spending quality time with a warrior goddess was really what she needed. "I'm not sure," she said, but Keisha was already nodding her head.

"Come on, Amanda," Sam urged her. "She's perfect. I mean, seriously, she's the goddess of battles. Who better to help you win a student council race?"

"Well," Amanda hedged, still thinking it over.

"I think Sam might be right," Keisha said. "I

mean, she's a *goddess*—she should be able to do just about anything, right?"

"Sure, and she's great to have on your side in a war," Sam said.

Amanda groaned. "This isn't a war, Sam. It's a student council race."

"Same thing," Sam replied with a shrug. Then he raised his eyebrows and looked Amanda directly in the eye. "She was a strong, independent woman in a world ruled by men. Doesn't that sound like someone you'd like to meet?"

Amanda sighed. Sam knew her way too well. He knew she idolized strong women like Susan B. Anthony, Harriet Tubman, and Eleanor Roosevelt. Of course, she'd never really been into Norse mythology, but maybe Freyja was the right woman for the job. Amanda glanced at the clock. Keisha's mom was going to be back soon, so if they were going to make a move, they needed to be quick about it.

She gazed back down at the picture, taking in Freyja's cool stare. Maybe Keisha and Sam were right. Maybe the goddess of battle—and love and wealth and whatever—was the way to go. After all, who else were they going to find in this book? *Rapunzel?* Somehow, Amanda didn't think a long-haired, tower-bound princess would be much help to her.

"Okay," Amanda said, looking at her friends. "Let's do it."

"Yeah!" Sam said, smiling with excitement.

Keisha clapped her hands together. "I can't wait to see her," she said. "I bet she's really cool. I just hope this works!"

With a deep breath, Amanda passed her left wrist over the picture, allowing the bracelet to just graze it. There was an odd stillness in the air, like nothing had changed.

Suddenly, there was a blinding flash, so bright that Amanda and her friends had to shield their eyes. When it had passed, they stood there for a few seconds blinking, stunned.

"Well . . . did it work?" Keisha prompted.

Amanda looked back at the picture and felt her heart sink. Nothing had changed. The picture was exactly the same as before. Amanda shook her head. "Nothing!" She turned toward Keisha. "When you did this, the character came right out of the book, didn't she?"

"Uh-huh," Keisha replied.

"So, then, why didn't it work for me?" Amanda grumbled, feeling more hopeless than ever. "That Freyja lady is still sitting right there!"

Keisha leaned over the picture and studied it carefully. "I don't get it." She tapped her finger against her chin. "We got the flash. That's exactly what happened when I did it. How come—"

"Ouch!" Amanda yelled. A sudden, sharp stabbing pain in her ankle had taken her by surprise.

"What's wrong?"

"I'm not sure," Amanda said. But when she looked down at the floor, her mouth dropped into a shocked O shape. The magic *had* worked after all. Only it had gone dreadfully awry. Instead of seeing Freyja, goddess of battle, love, and wealth, Amanda saw a two-inch-tall Viking charging at her with his spear aimed straight at her ankle.

CHAPTER
Three

"Hey! Quit it," Amanda yelled, sidestepping the Viking's charge so that his spear clanged into a metal desk leg instead of hers.

"Cursed beast!" he yelled. "I'll have you yet!" He charged a third time, but Amanda moved her leg out of the way so that he went sprawling across the pale beige carpet.

"What is *he* doing here?" she demanded, glancing up at her friends. She'd expected them to be as disappointed about the mix-up as she was, but instead Keisha and Sam were both looking at her as if she'd sprouted a second head.

"He *who*?" Sam asked.

"He *him*," Amanda replied, pointing down at the Viking, who was dusting himself off and getting ready to double back for another attack.

"Are you feeling okay, Amanda?" Keisha asked, placing a palm to her friend's forehead.

"*I'm* fine," Amanda said, "but you two are blind! Can't you see that little . . . Viking guy down there? He keeps trying to spear my ankle."

Both Keisha and Sam searched the floor with their eyes, their gazes passing right over the tiny figure without seeing him.

"I'm not imagining him," Amanda said in her defense. "Look! I've got a little scratch on my ankle where he hit me." She lifted her foot, and both Keisha and Sam examined the nick.

"But where is he?" Sam asked.

"Right there!" Amanda exclaimed, sidestepping him just in time.

"I don't get it," Keisha said. "Why can't we see him? You guys both saw the girl I brought out of the—oww!" Keisha yelled, grabbing at her foot. "I think he just speared me!"

Sure enough, when Amanda glanced down, the Viking was standing right next to Keisha, getting ready to charge her other foot. "Keisha, look out!" she cried, but she was too late.

"Hey!" Keisha shouted, jumping up onto her mother's chair and rubbing at both of her feet.

"Make him stop!" Meanwhile, down on the floor, the Viking had turned his attention to Sam's feet.

"He's coming your way," Amanda warned him, but Sam didn't move.

"I'm wearing wool socks," he said. "These things are so thick, there's no way he could get through—ahh! Why, you little—"

"We have to trap him," Amanda said. "He's only a couple of inches tall."

"Here," Sam said. He picked up a wicker wastebasket and removed its plastic trash bag. "Put this over him," he said, tossing it to Amanda.

Amanda caught the basket and plunked it down on the Viking, who had been getting ready to mount a second assault on Sam. "There!" she said. "Got him."

"What madness is this?" the Viking yelled, peering out through a hole in the wicker weave. It was so absurd—this tiny, metal-helmeted head poking out the side of an overturned wastebasket—that Amanda almost giggled. Until the Viking gripped the side of his makeshift prison and began to lift it. He may have been small, but he sure was strong.

"Quick! The book!" Amanda yelled. Keisha, who was still perched on her mother's chair, picked it up and handed it to Amanda, who placed it on top of the basket. Thankfully, its weight was enough to thwart the Viking's attempted escape.

"Is he trapped?" Keisha asked.

Amanda watched for a moment to be sure. There was a rattling coming from inside the trashbasket, but it stood motionless. Amanda nodded.

"Are you sure?" Keisha said from her perch.

"Yes, I'm sure," Amanda replied. "Gosh, Keisha. He's only this big." She held her thumb and forefinger out to demonstrate. "It's not like he's going to do any serious damage."

"I know," Keisha said, slowly stepping down from the chair. "It's just weird not being able to see him or anything."

"Yeah, I wonder why that is," Sam said.

"I don't know," Amanda replied. "We saw the girl Keisha brought out."

"Yeah, but you and Sam both had a connection to her," Keisha said thoughtfully. "You know, because it was Amanda's grandmother's book, and you guys had read that story so many times."

Amanda nodded. "I bet you're right. I don't think I ever read this Viking story. I don't even know what it's about."

"I *would* have read it," Sam said, "but Amanda never let me choose the stories. Maybe if you had, I'd be able to see him," he added, shooting Amanda a mock scowl.

"Whatever," Amanda said, rolling her eyes. "Either way, he's here, and now we've got to figure out what to do with him."

Slowly, Amanda, Sam, and Keisha crouched down around the wicker wastebasket and peered inside.

Amanda, of course, could see the Viking inside feeling at the walls of his new prison and trying to make sense of it, but to Keisha and Sam, it was just a disappointingly empty wicker basket.

"What's he doing?" Keisha asked. "Is he still trying to spear stuff?"

At the sound of her voice, the Viking turned toward her and Amanda, who were crowded on one side of the trash basket. "Maidens?" he said, sounding a bit confused. "Great Odin!" he exclaimed, gazing out at them. "Fair maidens, large as the skies! Am I dead? Is this . . . Valhalla?"

Amanda screwed up her face. "He wants to know if this is Valhalla," she said, glancing at Sam.

"He wants to know if he's *where*?" Keisha asked.

"Valhalla," Sam said. "It's like Viking heaven."

"Oh," Amanda said. She looked back at the tiny Viking. "Not exactly," she told him. "This is Boston."

"Boston," the Viking repeated. He glanced around outside his wicker cell, taking in the walls, the clock, the bookshelves, the file cabinet, which must have seemed immense to someone so small. "I'll say one thing for this Boston: It's a strange place. I've never seen anything like it. How did I get here?"

"I'm not sure exactly," Amanda said. "But I think I might have brought you."

"*You* brought me here?" the Viking said. He scratched at his beard. "By what magic? Last I remember, I was sailing the high seas, searching for new land."

Sam grabbed the book from the top of the wastebasket and flipped it open. "He must have been right here," he said, pointing at the picture of Freyja and the ships. "There was a Viking with a long red beard and a fur cape standing at the helm of this first ship, but he's gone now."

Amanda examined the Viking in the over-turned basket. With a full head of bushy red hair protruding from under his metal helmet, and a long fur cape on his back, he matched Sam's description perfectly. "Good eyes, Sam," she said. "That's the one. But how did I get him?"

"Maybe the bracelet brushed against him before it touched Freyja," Keisha suggested.

"Freyja!" the Viking exclaimed, staring at Amanda. "Of course! I was thrown at first because your hair is the wrong color, but yes," he squinted at her eyes. "I can see it now, you have the same slightly fierce look about the eyes. You must be she!" He paced back and forth inside his prison, gesticulating madly with his hands. "That's it! It all makes sense now! I must have died fighting that strange beast that appeared from out of the fog, and now you've brought me to your palace—your *Boston*—to celebrate my heroics."

"Uh . . . not exactly," Amanda said. "My name is Amanda, not Freyja," she told the tiny Viking. "And that beast you were fighting was my foot."

The Viking stopped pacing and scowled at Amanda. "Your . . . *foot*?"

"Mm-hm," Amanda nodded. "And my friends' feet, too," she added. "You charged all of us. You were kind of . . . excited."

For a moment the Viking appeared confused, but then he puffed out his chest. "I'm a warrior," he said proudly. "My name is Ulf, and I am greatly feared and respected in villages far and wide."

Amanda raised her eyebrows. "Your name is Elf?"

"Not *Elf*!" the Viking spat. "Ulf! Ulf the Red, a fierce warrior—"

"Yeah, I got that part," Amanda said.

"What's going on?" Sam asked. "What's he saying?"

The Viking cupped his hands in front of his mouth. "I said my name is Ulf the Red!" he bellowed. "I am a fierce warrior, feared and respected by—"

"Hey! I heard you the first time," Amanda told him, covering her ears.

"But the lad didn't."

"He can't. And neither can she," Amanda said, pointing at Keisha. "I brought you here, and I'm the only one who can hear or see you."

The Viking gave her a puzzled look. "That is not good," he muttered.

"Sorry," Amanda said. "I can't do anything about it."

Ulf furrowed his brow so deeply that his bushy eyebrows nearly joined together. He seemed to be thinking things over. After a moment, he took off his helmet and nodded to Amanda. "Well, then, if there's nothing to be done about it, I give you permission to act as my interpreter. You may tell them what I have said," he added with a flourish of his hand.

Amanda scowled at the Viking. Did he think she was his servant or something? Grudgingly, she looked up at her friends. "He said his name is Ulf the Red."

"Ulf the Red?" Sam asked, his eyes wide. He was obviously psyched to have a real, live Viking in the room—even if he couldn't see him.

"That's what he said."

"Tell them I am a fierce warrior, feared and respected by—"

"They don't need to know that," Amanda said, cutting him off.

"Know what?" Keisha asked.

Amanda rolled her eyes. "He says he's a fierce warrior, feared and respected by all," she repeated. As she spoke, Ulf stood erect, as though he were being introduced at a royal ball, and when Amanda finished, he bowed. "They can't see you," Amanda reminded him.

"I'm being polite," Ulf replied. "Just because I'm a berserker, it doesn't mean I haven't got manners."

"Did you say *berserker*?" Amanda asked. The Viking nodded. "What's that?"

"Whoa! He's a berserker?" Sam exclaimed. "That's amazing!"

"What's a berserker?" Keisha and Amanda asked at the same time.

"Only the fiercest kind of Viking warrior ever," Sam said. He ran a hand through his crazy hair and shook his head. "I should have known. He's wearing a fur cape, right?"

"Yeah," Amanda said.

"Well, that's where berserkers got their name, from wearing fur shirts or capes or whatever. It comes from the Norse words for bear shirt—*ber serkr*, or *berserker*, see?" Sam was getting excited now. He was talking faster and faster and his voice kept getting louder. "Berserkers were, like, totally crazy in combat. They'd spend hours before a battle dancing around and howling and stuff, really working themselves into a frenzy, and then they'd go insane on whole villages, spearing people left and right!"

"In self-defense," Ulf protested. "We only use our spears in self-defense." He dug a piece of dirt out from under one of his fingernails and flicked it onto the floor. "More or less."

"Some people think berserkers might actually have had extra-big heads that caused them pain, and that's why they were so aggressive," Sam went on.

"Big heads? Does the lad think I have a big head?" Ulf demanded. His fiery eyes were trained on Sam, and he was gripping his spear tightly in his left hand. Unless Amanda wanted him to charge again, she had to think quick.

"No, he doesn't think you have a big head," she told Ulf while giving Sam a say-another-word-and-I'll-smack-you look. "He can't see you, remember? He just has a vivid imagination."

The Viking scrutinized Amanda's face for a moment and then relaxed his grip on his spear. He paced a few times in his cell, considering what he had heard, and looked up at Amanda. "A good imagination is a fine thing," he said. "You have to have one to survive in this world. Why, I never would have gone on any journeys at all if I hadn't been able to imagine the riches they would lead to—jewels, gems, gold! And a better life for my people, of course," he added as an afterthought. Then he turned to Amanda and nodded. "You may tell the lad what I have said."

Amanda sighed. She was already tiring of her new friend. Nevertheless, she repeated his message to Sam, who grinned like a madman.

"Thank you, sir," Sam said, aiming his words in the general direction of the wicker wastepaper basket. "Hey, Amanda, we can probably let him out of there now, don't you think? I mean, he's not going to try to attack us anymore, is he?"

"I don't know. Are you?" Amanda asked the Viking.

"What do you think I am? A heathen?" he asked.

Amanda decided she was better off not answering that question. Instead, she lifted the wastebasket and passed it to Sam, who replaced its plastic liner.

"Ahh, that's better," Ulf said, taking a deep breath, sticking out his chest, and walking around in a big circle. While the Viking enjoyed his newfound freedom, Amanda looked to her friends.

"So?" she said. "What are we going to do with him?"

"What do you mean?" Keisha asked.

Amanda raised her hand in front of her mouth and whispered, "Personally, I think we should put him back in the book and try for the goddess."

"No way!" Sam shouted. "He's perfect! He's a Viking warrior—a berserker!—skilled at the art of battle and an excellent strategic planner. He'll definitely be able to help you win."

Hearing this, Ulf glanced up proudly, clutching his pike at his side and striking several theatric battle poses. "Win? I've never lost a fight in my life," he said. "Just show me where the battle is and I'm on my way."

"It's not like that," Amanda said. "I'm not waging a war. I'm just running for student council."

Ulf nodded thoughtfully. "A seat on the high council is a very respectable position. I served on a high council—until I got into a fight with the chief and was exiled from the village." He chewed at his thumbnail for a minute and then spit something on the ground.

"Oh, no," Amanda groaned. She was about to explain to Keisha and Sam just how unqualified the Viking was to help when the office door suddenly swung open.

"There you are!" Mrs. Johnson said, standing in the doorway with one hand on her hip. "I've been looking all over the store. What are you doing back here with the door closed and the lights off? Can you even *see* the register, Keisha?"

"Of course I can," Keisha said. "I've been watching through the window."

Mrs. Johnson stared at the three kids with narrowed eyes, scrutinizing each of their faces. Then she focused on Keisha. "The next time I ask you to keep an eye on the register, I expect you to keep the door open," she said finally. "Okay?"

"No problem, Mom. Sorry," Keisha replied.

Mrs. Johnson held her daughter's gaze for another moment before turning to Amanda.

"Your mother is here to pick up you and Sam," she said. "She's waiting outside."

"Oh. Okay," Amanda said. She glanced down at the tiny Viking, wondering what she was going to do with him, and decided she'd have to figure it out later. As she stood, she scooped Ulf up in one hand and tucked him into the pocket of her secondhand blue velour warm-up jacket.

"What's this? Unhand me, woman!" Ulf shouted as he tumbled deep into her pocket. Amanda reached in and carefully extracted his spear from his hands, placing it in her other pocket. She could handle him bouncing around, but she didn't need him jabbing at her all the way home.

"See you later, Keisha," Amanda said as she grabbed her backpack. "I'll give you a call tonight. Oh, hey—do you mind if I borrow this?" she asked, picking up the book. "I'd kind of like to read that Viking story."

"Sure," Keisha said with a grin.

Amanda knelt down and opened her back-pack, somehow managing to wedge the book of fairy tales inside. Her bag was already heavy with homework—math, science, language arts, social studies, even music.

"Let me out of here!" Ulf yelled from her pocket. "I'm a warrior! I'll have your head!"

Amanda sighed as she and Sam walked toward her mom's car. Something told her it was going to be a long night.

CHAPTER
Four

"Okay, look," Amanda said, dumping the Viking out of her pocket and onto her blue-and-white-striped bedspread. "I'm the only one who can hear or see you around here, so you're going to have to cooperate with me. That means no more yelling and screaming, all right?"

"You tried to smother me!" the Viking protested.

"I did *not* try to smother you," Amanda said. "I put you in my pocket to get you home, that's all."

"A maiden's pocket is no place for a ship's captain!" Ulf shouted.

"Be quiet!" Amanda said, staring him down.

The Viking held her gaze for a moment,

then, in a huff, turned and stalked off across her bed. "Quiet," he said, "is not in my nature. I am a warrior. I do not sit back and wait for things to happen—*I* go out and happen to *things*."

"Not here, you don't," Amanda said. Ulf looked up at her, defiant, but she wasn't backing down. "In case you haven't noticed, you're, like, one-tenth the size of—"

"Vile demon!" Ulf called out, thrusting his spear into the air. Amanda barely had time to react. In a nanosecond, the Viking had slid down her comforter, landing on the floor with his spear in striking position.

"Ulf! What are you—?" Amanda started, but then she saw the cause of the commotion. Her cat, Frodo, had pushed open her door and entered the room. Frodo was a ginger cat with long hair, and apparently Ulf had mistaken him for some sort of dangerous beast, which, Amanda realized, he probably was to Ulf. Frodo was easily ten times the Viking's size.

"Prepare to meet your maker!" Ulf bellowed, charging at Frodo with his spear extended in front of him.

"Ulf! Stop!" Amanda yelled. She stepped forward, preparing to lift her cat out of harm's way, but Frodo had puffed up his fur and was now hissing in Ulf's general direction. The cat wasn't looking directly at Ulf, but it was close enough that Amanda could tell he at least sensed the Viking's presence.

Frodo hissed, but Ulf was undaunted. He continued his charge despite the fact that Frodo had lifted one of his paws, claws fully extended.

"Are you crazy?" Amanda said, lunging for the Viking. "He'll shred you!"

"Not without a fight, he won't," Ulf declared. He dodged Amanda and charged at Frodo, stabbing his spear into the cat's raised paw. Frodo yowled in pain, then held his wounded paw up and cocked his head, obviously confused. He couldn't see the little Viking, but he had certainly felt him.

"Ulf, stop it!" Amanda cried, concerned about her cat, but Frodo was far from backing down. Just as Ulf was about to jab him again, Frodo made a wide swat at the air with his paw.

Ulf ducked just in time. "You'll have to be quicker than that!" he called with a hearty laugh. As if he had heard, Frodo hissed in return and swatted at the Viking again, this time managing to cuff Ulf on the shoulder.

"Great Odin!" Ulf cried. "This monster has claws like daggers!"

"Ulf, get over here!" Amanda ordered him. She stepped forward and made another grab at the Viking. This time he dodged her by running straight at Frodo and making a leap for the cat's side. Clutching thick clumps of ginger fur in his tiny fists, Ulf clung to Frodo, managing to swing one leg over the cat's back. Frodo thrashed his tail madly and twisted his head around, trying to nip at his back.

"Your fangs don't frighten me, mongrel!" Ulf cried, riding the cat as if he were competing in a rodeo.

Amanda looked on in horror, alternately yelling at Ulf for jabbing at Frodo and then at Frodo for trying to bite Ulf, and periodically making tentative grabs for the Viking. After all, she didn't want to get stabbed, clawed, or bitten. But when Ulf seized Frodo's collar in one hand and lifted his spear in the other, Amanda knew she had to act fast.

"Frodo!" she yelled, and she clapped her hands together as loudly as she could. The cat, surprised by the sudden loud noise, crouched for a moment then bolted under Amanda's bed.

Fortunately—for the cat, not for Ulf—the bed was fairly low to the floor and Ulf was caught off guard. Instead of stabbing his spear into the cat's neck as he had planned, the Viking was knocked backward when his helmet banged against the metal bed rail.

Quickly, Amanda swooped in and picked up the Viking, who was lying flat on his back and moaning.

"What were you thinking?" Amanda demanded, but Ulf was in no condition to answer.

With the Viking temporarily disabled, Amanda turned her attention to the cat. "Out, Frodo!" she commanded, pulling him out from under the bed by his collar and shooing him toward the door with her foot.

As Frodo exited, Ulf came to and tried to wriggle out of Amanda's grip. "Where's that beast? I'm not finished with him yet. Get him back in here and I'll—"

"—stay right where you are," Amanda said, setting Ulf back on the bed. "And chill out," she added. "You got lucky, you know. That cat could have torn you to pieces."

"You underestimate my skill in battle," the Viking told her.

"Yeah, and you overestimate your size," Amanda replied.

Ulf threw his shoulders back. "I'll have you know that I—"

"Yeah, yeah. You're a fierce warrior, feared by all. I got it," Amanda said. "Thing is, that *beast* happens to be my pet cat and I—"

"That mongrel is your pet?" Ulf exclaimed.

Amanda looked at the Viking with his wild red hair and long beard. He was probably a pretty fierce man in his time, but at two inches, he was kind of hard to take seriously. "Yes, he is," Amanda said. "And I'd like to keep him—and you—in one piece. So do you think you can find something to do for the next hour that doesn't involve attacking anything?"

The Viking glanced toward the door, gripping his spear tightly. Pursuing Frodo was obviously on his mind. But he took a few deep breaths, frowned, sighed, and finally gazed back at Amanda.

"Fine," he said. "I'll do some training. A warrior has to keep himself in prime physical condition."

"O-kay," Amanda said, though it didn't seem to her that Ulf, with his large gut and meaty hands, was anywhere near being in prime physical condition. Still, she was happy to have the little Viking occupied for a bit while she tackled her homework, and training sounded harmless enough. A few sit-ups, some push-ups, maybe even some sprints. Ulf was so small that her bedroom would be like a stadium to him.

Amanda pulled her social studies text from her backpack and settled down at her desk. The chapter Mrs. MacKnight had assigned for homework was on agriculture in Mesopotamia. Amanda tried hard to focus on the words in front of her, but she was having a hard time concentrating. Partly because the textbook was so boring, and partly because of the loud knocking noise coming from the other side of her bed.

She sprang from her desk chair and leaped onto her bed, peering over the far edge. "Ulf! What are you doing?!"

"Just a little target practice," the Viking replied, wrenching his spear from the wall.

Amanda stared at the numerous tiny holes just above her baseboard. "Ulf! You—"

"I know," the Viking said proudly. "Twelve perfect shots. I told you I was a mighty warrior."

"Yeah," Amanda said. She dropped her head into her hands, wondering how she was going to explain all the marks in her wall to her mother. "You're something, all right."

The cuckoo clock in the living room woke Amanda at midnight, as usual. Normally, she would have stirred slightly, mumbled, "Just the clock," and fallen back to sleep. But tonight she had a plan.

She swung her legs out of bed and crept over to her jewelry box, which she had emptied to make a bed for the Viking. "Ulf," she whispered, careful to keep her voice quiet. The Viking didn't stir. "Ulf!" Amanda repeated, making her voice just the slightest bit louder. Still no response.

"Nice," Amanda sighed, relaxing a bit. She watched the Viking sleep for a moment, his tiny chest rising and falling in rhythm with the sound of his breath. *All right*, Amanda thought. *It's now or never.*

Carefully, she maneuvered her hand underneath the tiny Viking and scooped him up as gently as she could.

"Land! Off the starboard side!" Ulf bellowed suddenly.

Amanda gasped, almost dropping him, but somehow she managed to hold on. As she watched, the Viking turned over in her hand, readjusting himself and falling back into a deep slumber.

Just talking in his sleep, Amanda reassured herself as the Viking began snoring. Slowly, Amanda carried him over to her desk, where she had left the book of fairy tales before going to sleep. It was already open to the picture of the Viking; Amanda had made sure of that.

Gently, she set Ulf down just above his ship, and once again he rolled over. "Hoist the mainsail!" he called. "Row, on my count!" Amanda held her breath and waited. Once again, Ulf readjusted himself, lying on his side and curling his knees up to his chest, and once again, he fell back into a deep sleep.

"Phew," Amanda whispered, one hand on her chest. His two small outbursts had sent her heart rate soaring, but thankfully he hadn't been disturbed at all. Evidently, Ulf was a very heavy sleeper.

"Okay," Amanda murmured, "just lie still. Here we go." She raised her left hand and passed the charm bracelet over the page, touching it to the sail of the Viking ship. Then she waited, watching the picture expectantly, but nothing happened. The picture stayed the same and Ulf continued to lie on top of it, snoring away.

Maybe I missed, Amanda thought. Again she passed the bracelet over the picture, being careful to touch each of the charms to Ulf's ship, but again nothing happened.

"What the—?" Amanda muttered. She lowered her wrist onto the page and pressed the bracelet into the picture—softly at first, and then as hard as she could. Still, nothing happened. No swirling of the picture, no blinding flash of light.

Am I doing something wrong? Amanda wondered, but if she was, she had no idea what it could be.

"Ready the battering ram!" Ulf cried out, shifting in his sleep once again.

"Great," Amanda muttered, gazing at the bushy-haired, bearded Viking lying before her. "I'm running for student council and I'm stuck with Attila the Hun as my campaign manager."

CHAPTER
Five

"Did you bring him?" Sam asked as he set his lunch tray across from Amanda's and Keisha's.

Amanda nodded. She hadn't wanted to bring Ulf to school with her, but leaving him at home with Frodo didn't seem like such a great idea, either. One of them was sure to end up hurt by the end of the day, and even though Ulf was only two inches tall, Amanda wasn't totally sure her cat would win!

"Where is he?" Sam asked.

"He's right there," Amanda said, pointing with her fork. "Gnawing on my roll. He doesn't trust any of the other food I got for him."

Ulf was sitting on the edge of Amanda's lunch tray with the roll resting in front of him like a huge boulder. Next to the roll, Amanda had set a few French fries and a chicken nugget that she'd scrounged from Keisha, but Ulf hadn't touched them. "Great Odin! And why shouldn't I be wary? What is this thing, anyway?" he asked, kicking at the nugget.

"It's chicken," Amanda said.

"Chicken? And just what part of the chicken is it, eh? I've seen plenty of chickens in my life, but never one with a wing or a leg shaped like this." With a mighty leap, Ulf jumped onto the nugget and bounced up and down a few times before landing back on the table. Then, with great effort, he picked up the perfectly round breaded nugget and heaved it across Amanda's tray.

"Whoa! Incoming poultry!" Sam cried, watching the nugget fly. "Did Ulf do that?"

Amanda scowled. "Yes. He doesn't believe it's really chicken because it doesn't look like a drumstick or a wing or anything."

"If we gave him a real drumstick, it would be five times his size," Sam said.

Ulf licked his lips. "I could eat off of it for a week," he said, his eyes glittering with excitement. "And that creature we saw this morning," he went on, still drooling. "Its meat could feed my entire family for a month."

"I already told you—Mr. Fluffy is off-limits,"

Amanda said. Mr. Fluffy was the class guinea pig, and during language arts class, Ulf had expressed quite an interest in the possibility of roasting him for dinner. "And so is Frodo," Amanda added.

Keisha's eyebrows shot up. "He wants to eat Mr. Fluffy? And your cat?"

"He wants to eat everything," Amanda replied, rolling her eyes.

"Not this flotsam," Ulf said, gesturing toward the food Amanda had given him. "Never trust meat you haven't killed yourself—that's my rule. This bread is the only thing here that resembles anything like food, if you ask me."

"No one did," Amanda replied, rolling her eyes for the tenth time in the last hour. She grabbed one of Ulf's fries and shoved it into her mouth, following it with a sip of milk.

Ulf snorted and grinned as he ripped off another chunk of bread. "You're a fiery one," he muttered, shoving the food into his mouth. Amanda watched in disgust. His red beard was already flecked with bread crumbs and droplets of the milk. She'd managed to fashion Ulf a glass from a pen cap by breaking off its long tab and propping it up at the side of the tray, but now she was thinking her time would have been better spent making him a bib. "Ah, what I wouldn't give for leg of mutton or a nice horse skewer," Ulf said, wiping his face with his arm.

Amanda couldn't take any more. "Look, Ulf, you need to stop talking with your mouth full. You're spitting food all over the place. There's already a bunch of stuff stuck in your beard."

Keisha grimaced. "Ew. I'm glad I can't see *that*," she said.

Ulf paused for a moment and stared up at Amanda. Then he threw his head back and gave a hearty laugh. "You sound just like my mother, rest her soul," he said. Then he went back to eating with renewed vigor.

Amanda cocked her head and scowled. She wasn't trying to sound like anyone's mother. She was just trying to keep her lunch down.

"It's going to be so cool to be on the student council," an approaching voice said.

And that's not going to help, Amanda thought. Looking up, she saw Jenna and her two devoted lackeys, Emily and Sarah, headed up to dump their trays.

"Yeah, once you're elected, you can help plan dances and stuff," Sarah said.

"And they'll be way better than the one we had last week," Emily added.

"With cooler decorations," Jenna put in, glancing over at Amanda, Keisha, and Sam.

"Oh, brother," Amanda mumbled. She was tempted to speak up, but she knew Jenna was just trying to upset them.

Unfortunately, Keisha couldn't let it go. "People loved our decorations!" she blurted.

Jenna stopped at the end of their table and smirked. "Oh, your decorations were cute, for sure," she said sweetly. "But this is middle school—not nursery school."

Keisha bristled, and Amanda touched her elbow in an attempt to calm her down. There was no point in arguing with Jenna. She was just trying to get a reaction from them, anyway. But Keisha was already too wound up. "What's that supposed to mean?" she asked.

"Just that elephants and monkeys are kind of lame for a middle school dance," Jenna replied.

"Jenna's going to make sure the holiday dance is semiformal," Emily said, stepping closer to the table and wearing a smirk that was practically identical to Jenna's. *She's probably been practicing it in the mirror*, Amanda thought.

"Isn't the student council planning the holiday dance?" Sam asked.

"Mm-hm," Jenna said with a nod.

"But you're not on the student council," Keisha protested.

"I will be," Jenna replied.

"Hmph. She's a fiery one, too," Ulf observed, spitting more bread crumbs into his beard. Amanda wrinkled her nose at him and he wiped his chin with his sleeve. "Hard habit to break," he told her, but Amanda just shook her head. *Some lunch.* Ulf was disgusting, and Jenna was repulsive. The conditions weren't exactly ideal for eating. Amanda decided to concentrate on scraping the ketchup on her plate into one lump while she waited for Ulf to finish and Jenna to leave.

"How can you say that?" Keisha demanded. There was such venom in her voice that Amanda forgot about her ketchup for a moment and looked up. She knew there was no point in arguing with Jenna. Jenna was too stuck on herself to see anyone else's point of view, and it would be best if Keisha could just learn to ignore her. Still, Amanda had to admit, it was nice to hear her friend sticking up for her.

"Easy. I don't have any competition," Jenna said.

"Yes, you do!" Keisha spat. Amanda shifted

her gaze back to her plate, aware that she was beginning to blush. Keisha's fierce loyalty was becoming a little embarrassing. "Of course you have competition," Keisha went on. "What do you call Noah Carpenter?"

For a moment Jenna looked surprised. Then she laughed. "*Noah?* That's funny. I thought you were talking about your new best friend," she said, nodding at Amanda.

So did I, Amanda thought bitterly.

Jenna turned to Emily and Sarah. "Isn't that sad?" she said. "Not even her friends think she has a chance." The three girls laughed as they walked away, and Amanda frowned at Keisha.

"I didn't mean—" Keisha started. "It's not that I don't think—shoot! Why do I always let her get to me like that? I was just trying to tell her that she's not the only popular person running. Not that you're not popular," she added quickly. "What I mean is—"

"It's okay, Keisha," Amanda interrupted. "I'm *not* popular. And you're right. Aside from Noah, Jenna doesn't have any competition. I don't know why I let you guys talk me into this."

"Because of the bracelet," Sam reminded her. "We have magic on our side. And Ulf," he added, pointing toward Amanda's dinner roll, which looked as if a mouse had been gnawing on it.

"Yeah, maybe he can help," Keisha suggested.

"I doubt it," Amanda said. "Unless there's some kind of eating contest involved." She glanced down at the Viking, who was still shoving bits of bread into his mouth. Small as he was, he'd already devoured half the roll.

"Ask him," Sam urged. "Maybe there's something he can do."

"Find out if he can do magic," Keisha suggested.

Amanda sighed. The only magic Ulf seemed capable of was making food disappear. But if her friends wanted her to ask, she'd ask.

"Hey, Ulf," she said. The Viking continued to grunt and chew. "Oh, brother," Amanda mumbled. "Ulf!" she called, louder this time.

"Hm?" Ulf wiped his mouth on his sleeve again and picked up the pen cap. "I could use a bit more milk in my cup," he said, licking his lips.

"Fine," Amanda replied. She took the pen cap from him and refilled it.

Ulf took a big swig from the cap. "Ahhh," he said, wiping his mouth on his sleeve once again. He started to rip off another chunk of bread, but stopped mid-tear. "Was there something you wanted to ask me?"

Amanda glanced at her friends, who were looking on hopefully. "Yeah. We were wondering—can you do magic?"

Ulf stood up and stared at Amanda with his furry eyebrows knit together. "Magic?" he bellowed. "You mean *witchcraft?* What do you take me for, girl? A leprechaun?"

"What did he say?" Sam asked.

"He says he's an explorer, not an elf," Amanda informed her friends.

"Oh, hey, Ulf," Sam said, gazing at the half-eaten roll. "Don't be upset. We know you're a great explorer and a fierce warrior and everything. It's just that the bracelet Amanda's wearing is magic, and we thought maybe some of the magic rubbed off on you."

Ulf sat back down and stroked his beard. Sam glanced hopefully at Amanda, but she just shrugged her shoulders. The Viking seemed to have calmed down, but she had no idea what he was thinking. Finally, after about fifteen seconds, he stood up again.

"Perhaps the lad is right. Perhaps I do have some magic. But how can I find out?"

"I'm not sure," Amanda said. "I guess you could point your stick at something—"

"It's a spear!" Ulf interrupted. "What earthly good would a stick do me in battle?"

"*Sor*-ry," Amanda said. For a medieval warrior, he sure was touchy about his terminology. "Okay, then. Point your *spear* at something and, I don't know, try to . . . make it move."

"Say some magic words," Sam put in.

"Yeah, like *abracadabra*," Keisha suggested.

"Very well." Ulf took a step away from the dinner roll he'd been munching on so greedily, pointed his spear at it, and in a thunderous voice called out, "Up, great loaf! Up!" He held his arm out rigidly, shaking with the effort, but no matter how high he lifted his spear, the dinner roll stayed right where it was.

With a violent exhalation, Ulf let his arm fall and turned back to Amanda. "No luck," he told her.

"Obviously," Amanda said. She frowned at the roll and thought for a second. "What if you try something without the spear?" she suggested. "Like, you could think about something that you really want and try to make it appear."

"All right," Ulf said. "I'll give it a try." He set

his spear on the tray and stood up, crossing his arms over his chest and closing his eyes. "Let's see . . . I want a plump goat, skewered and roasting over a fire and—"

"Uhh! That's gross," Amanda interrupted.

"You said I should think about something I want," the Viking protested, his large hands on his hips.

"I know, but can't you think of something that doesn't involve food?" Amanda asked. "Isn't there anything you want that doesn't have to be killed and cooked first?"

Ulf knit his substantial eyebrows together and scratched his beard. Then suddenly, he brightened. "My woolly-woolly!" he said with a smile.

"Your *what*?"

"My woolly-woolly," Ulf replied with a far-away look. "It's a doll my mother stitched for me using leftover fleece. She gave it to me when I was just wee one and I took it everywhere with me." Ulf folded his arms together as if cradling a baby, and Amanda raised her eyebrows. This was a side of the Viking she hadn't seen before.

"Naturally, I gave it up when I turned four," Ulf added gruffly. "A boy has to become a man, you know. But still, I loved my woolly-woolly while I had him."

A woolly-woolly, Amanda thought. *Much better than a roasted goat.* "Okay," she said. "Give it a try."

Again, Ulf closed his eyes, but this time he was silent. Instead of speaking, he just stood there mouthing words to himself and smiling every now and then.

Amanda glanced over at Sam and Keisha, who were staring at her expectantly. "He's trying to make his woolly-woolly appear," she whispered. Sam and Keisha gave her puzzled looks, but Amanda waved them off. "I'll explain later," she mouthed. Then she looked back at Ulf.

"Is he here?" Ulf asked hopefully. "Do you see him?" He ran around the back side of the dinner roll, then checked under the remaining fries and over the edge of the tray.

Amanda shook her head. "Doesn't look like it worked," she said. Then she turned to Sam and Keisha. "I don't think he can do magic," she told them.

Ulf walked to the back of the tray, slumped down behind his half-eaten roll, and sulked.

"Poor woolly-woolly," he mumbled. "I wonder what ever became of him."

Amanda ignored the Viking's pouting and continued talking to Sam and Keisha. "So that's that," she said. "I'm dropping out of the race this afternoon."

"Amanda!" Sam said.

"You can't!" Keisha declared.

"Race? What race?" Ulf asked, straightening up. "Whatever it is, I'm sure I can help you win." He grabbed his spear and walked toward Amanda, his sadness over his long-lost doll seemingly forgotten. "I'm swift as a river running to the sea!" he declared, and to prove his point, the tiny Viking started running sprints back and forth across Amanda's lunch tray, jabbing his spear at imaginary foes every time he reached the end.

"It's not that kind of race, Ulf," Amanda said. The Viking came skidding to a stop and turned to her with a bewildered look. "It's an election," Amanda explained.

"Ah, yes," he said, nodding. "I remember now. You want a seat on the high council."

"It's not the high council," Amanda corrected him. "It's the student council. And if I want to be on it, I have to get more votes than that girl who was just at the table."

"The fiery one?" Ulf asked.

"Yeah, her," Amanda said. "Which is impossible, so I'm dropping out."

"Nonsense," the Viking said. "You will not drop out. You will proceed and win."

"I *can't* win, Ulf," Amanda told him. "The other people running are way more popular than I am."

Ulf shook his head. "Don't be ignorant," he said. "Elections aren't about who is more socially appealing. They're about issues."

"Boy, you *are* from the Middle Ages, aren't you?" Amanda said, but Ulf ignored her.

"The way to win an election," he went on, "is to find out what the people want and offer it to them. That's how I got my high council seat, and that's how I got twenty-five ships full of people to follow me in search of new lands. I'm quite the diplomat," he said with a smug smile. "And if I can get people to uproot their families and risk their lives, don't you think I can help you win a few measly votes?"

Amanda narrowed her eyes. Without all that food in his mouth, the little Viking actually sounded fairly intelligent. "I guess," Amanda conceded.

Keisha and Sam, who had been listening in on Amanda's side of the conversation, noticed the change in her tone and perked up.

"Is he going to help?" Keisha asked.

"I knew he'd be perfect!" Sam said with a grin.

"What you need to do," Ulf went on, "is lay a little groundwork. You have to plant the seeds before you can reap the harvest, you know."

"What's that supposed to mean?" Amanda asked.

"It's simple," Ulf told her. "Nose around a bit. Talk to your friends. Find out what people are unhappy about and then promise them something better. That's all it ever takes."

Amanda stared at the Viking in surprise. Everything he was saying made sense, especially now that he wasn't spitting bread crumbs. Maybe the student council race *could* be about issues and not just popularity. And if that was the case, maybe Amanda did have a chance at getting elected.

"You know, Ulf, you're a pretty smart guy," Amanda said. Having the tiny Viking around might prove to be useful after all.

Ulf raised his pen cap of milk to her and took a big swig from it. When he finished, his beard was dotted with white droplets that had rained down from his milk-soaked mustache.

If only he could work on his hygiene.

CHAPTER
Six

This is impossible, Amanda thought. *I'm never going to come up with anything.*

By the end of math class, she'd filled two pages in her notebook with possible campaign platform ideas and crossed out every last one of them. Twice. Figuring out what her classmates wanted was no easy task. And Ulf wasn't making it any easier.

"More property," he kept insisting. "That's what people want. If you want votes, just promise them larger tracts of farmland. They'll follow you anywhere."

"We're sixth graders, not barons," Amanda had reminded him more than once, but Ulf couldn't seem to get his mind around the difference. Now, on their way to social studies class, he was suggesting that perhaps Amanda should appeal to her classmates by offering to let them keep their own livestock.

"I don't think handing out sheep is going to win me any votes," Amanda muttered as she took her seat.

Michelle Burton, who was sitting directly across from her, looked up. "What's that?" she asked, wrinkling her nose.

"Oh—nothing," Amanda said. "I was just . . . singing to myself," she managed. She caught Keisha's eye across the room and smiled. It would be easier to cover up her mutterings to Ulf if she and Keisha were in the same group, but unfortunately Amanda had been assigned to work with Michelle Burton and Corey Russell. They were putting together a diorama of the Assyrian Empire.

"Strange song," Michelle replied, twirling one of her short red curls around her pencil.

"Yeah, well, I like alternative music," Amanda said.

"Me, too," Corey said, taking his seat. "What group are you talking about?"

"Some band that sings about sheep," Michelle said.

Corey stared thoughtfully at the ceiling, his straight blond hair standing up in crisp spikes.

"I don't think I know them," he said finally. "What are they called?"

"The . . . Vikings," Amanda said.

"The Vikings?" Corey repeated.

"Yeah, they're from Norway," Amanda said, "so they're not very well known here."

"Oh," Corey said. And before he could ask any more questions, Amanda grabbed the box in which she, Michelle, and Corey had been creating their Assyrian scenes.

"So, anyway, what do we need to add to this thing to finish it?" Amanda asked. Both Corey and Michelle leaned in closer to examine their work. So far the box contained a few statues of important Assyrians, clay tablets on a shelf to represent a library, and a blue strip of cellophane that ran down the center to represent the Tigris River.

"We should probably do something with farming," Corey suggested.

"See? Farmland is important to everyone," Ulf started, but Amanda silenced him with a look. "Fine," he snarled. "I'll just go take a nap." He curled up on the corner of the table nearest Amanda and began to snore loudly.

"Great," Amanda sighed, resting her chin in her hands.

"What?" Corey asked. "They were farmers, you know."

"It's not that," Amanda said. "I just . . . have a headache."

"Maybe you should go to the school nurse," Michelle suggested, her blue eyes wide.

"No, it's not that bad. I'll be fine."

"Jill Brenner got a headache in gym the other day and she ended up going home sick. I think she had the flu or something," Michelle said.

"I don't have the flu," Amanda said. "I'm just—"

"Is everything all right over here?" Mrs. MacKnight interrupted, stopping beside their table. "How's your diorama coming?"

"Good," Amanda said. "We were just trying to decide what else to put in it."

Mrs. MacKnight eyed the three students suspiciously, then pushed her glasses up on her nose. "Just see that you stay on task," she told them. "Remember, this is class time—not gossip time." She fixed them with one last steely stare and continued her rounds.

"Sheesh. She's in one of her moods today, huh?" Corey whispered. Amanda and Michelle both nodded. They all had Mrs. MacKnight for both homeroom and social studies, and over the course of the school year, they'd learned that her moods were incredibly unpredictable. Most of the time, she was really nice. That morning, for instance, she'd brought in muffins for her entire homeroom. But at some point in the day, her mood apparently had switched, which meant that students needed to be on their best behavior or risk detention.

Of course, Amanda knew the moods had been brought on by a little magical mishap that Keisha had been involved with when *she'd* had the charm bracelet. But that didn't make the sudden swings any easier to deal with.

"I hate it when she's like this," Michelle said.

Amanda shrugged. "At least it doesn't happen too often."

"I guess," Michelle said. "But still, I like her a lot better when she's giving us cookies and stuff."

"Yeah, I could use a cookie today," Corey said. "Lunch was so short, I didn't even have time to finish eating. I'm starving."

"Me, too," Michelle said, still chewing on her pencil.

"Miss Burton! Are we on task?" Mrs. MacKnight called from across the room.

"Yes, Mrs. MacKnight," Michelle said, hunkering down over her work. "Man, what is it with teachers?" she whispered to Amanda and Corey. "It's like they expect us to work like robots from the minute we get to school until the minute we leave, without any breaks or anything."

"Except lunch," Amanda said.

"If you can call it that," Corey said. "Twenty minutes? I can barely get through the line in that time."

"Yeah, that's what stinks about sixth grade. And no more recess, either," Michelle complained.

Amanda saw Mrs. MacKnight approaching out of the corner of her eye and cleared her throat to alert her friends. "I think you're right about the farming, Corey," she said, louder than necessary. Ulf stirred slightly, but continued to snore. "We should try to put a field right here, next to this part of the river," she added, tapping the cellophane.

"And maybe an aqueduct," Michelle said, taking the hint. Mrs. MacKnight gave them a tight-lipped smile and kept moving.

"School is like prison," Corey muttered when she was gone.

"These sound like complaints to me," Ulf mumbled, still curled up on his side. Amanda narrowed her eyes. Wasn't he supposed to be sleeping? "Find out what the people want," Ulf added drowsily, and in another second he was snoring again.

What a weird little Viking, Amanda thought. But she had to give him credit. The stuff Michelle and Corey had mentioned—the short lunch period and the elimination of recess for middle schoolers—were things she'd heard other people complain about, too. In fact, Amanda had even complained about them herself.

But how could she possibly promise her classmates a longer lunch and a recess? It wasn't like teachers were going to shorten their classes just to help her win a student council seat.

Still, it was worth some thought. If she could come up with a way to offer those things to her classmates, it wouldn't matter how many semiformal dances Jenna Scott planned or how cute and popular Noah Carpenter was—everyone would be voting for Amanda Littlefield for student council.

CHAPTER
Seven

"What are you working on?" Keisha asked, looking over Amanda's shoulder. Amanda was propped up against the wall just inside the entryway to the school where she, Keisha, and Sam were waiting for her mother to pick them up.

"Yeah, you've been scribbling in that notebook for the last ten minutes," Sam said.

"Longer than that," Keisha told him. "She started at the end of social studies and kept going right through science and afternoon homeroom. Good thing Mrs. MacKnight's mood switched again or you'd be sitting in detention for ignoring the afternoon announcements."

Amanda sighed and let her pencil fall to the floor. "There has to be a way to make it work," she muttered.

"To make *what* work?" Sam and Keisha said together.

Amanda looked up at them and shook her head. "I'll tell you later," she said. "It's just an idea for the student council race, but I want to figure out if it will work before I talk about it." She'd been working on rearranging the school schedule so that different classes would get shortened to make room for a longer lunch and a recess, but she hadn't come up with anything she thought the teachers or the principal would go for.

"When's your mom supposed to be here, anyway?" Sam asked.

"Any time," Amanda said. "She probably just got stuck in traffic."

"I hope she's here soon," Keisha said. "I can't wait to get to Quincy Market. I love all the little shops! Can we stop at that cool jewelry stand?"

"I want to hit the CD Exchange," Sam said. "They're having a sale on used CDs—buy two, get one free—and I need some new music."

"We can do both," Amanda said. "My mom's meeting is supposed to last a couple of hours. We'll have plenty of time."

"Cool!" Keisha gushed. "I love walking

around the North End. It's so—" Suddenly, she stopped talking and began smoothing back her hair and checking her reflection in the glass of the entry door. It took Amanda only one glance over her shoulder to figure out why.

"Hey, Keisha," Noah said, sauntering over. He gave Keisha one of his lopsided grins, and Amanda almost groaned. Honestly. What did Keisha see in this guy? He was so arrogant. "Are you going to the pizza party tomorrow afternoon?"

Keisha wrinkled her nose. "What pizza party?"

"What do you mean 'what pizza party?' The one Jenna's parents are throwing. I thought everyone knew about it," Noah said.

"Yeah, well, I'm not exactly one of Jenna's best friends," Keisha said.

Noah shrugged. "That doesn't matter," he said. "The whole sixth grade is invited. Jenna got her parents to rent out Casa Napoli because she's running for student council."

This time Amanda did groan. "She rented out a pizza place? How am I supposed to compete with that?"

Noah squinted at her as if she'd interrupted

a private conversation, then turned back to Keisha. "What's up with her?" he asked, nodding toward Amanda.

"Amanda's running for student council, too," Keisha explained.

Again Noah turned toward Amanda, this time with a slight look of recognition. "Oh, right," he said. "So, anyway," he went on, "are you going to go?"

"I don't think so," Keisha said. "I'm not planning on voting for Jenna, so I probably shouldn't."

"I'm not voting for Jenna, either," Noah said with a smirk, "but I'm going. You should come."

Amanda watched as her friend's mouth curved into a shy smile. *Don't do it, Keisha,* she thought.

"I don't know," Keisha said. "Do you really think Jenna's inviting everyone?"

"Sure," Noah said. "She invited me and I'm running against her." Keisha bit her lip while she thought it over, and Noah added, "They could come, too, you know," gesturing toward Amanda and Sam.

Oh, how kind, Amanda thought. It was the

first time Noah had even acknowledged Sam, who was standing right next to Keisha.

"Well," Keisha started, and then she stole a glance at Amanda. It was at that moment Amanda realized that loyalty to her was the only thing that had stopped Keisha from jumping at the invitation already. And now she appeared to be looking for Amanda's approval.

"They're doing a buffet. It's all-you-can-eat," Noah added for extra incentive.

Just then, Ulf popped out of the front pocket of Amanda's backpack, where he'd been napping once again. "You have to go," he proclaimed, "for two reasons. Number one, it's always good to know what your enemy is up to. If this party is part of her strategy, you'd better be there to see how she uses it. And number two, you should never turn down free food."

Amanda wasn't so sure about the second reason, but she had to admit Ulf might be right about the first. If Jenna was inviting the whole sixth grade for pizza, Amanda should probably be there to see if she was making any campaign promises. She gave Keisha a shrug and then a nod, and Keisha's face brightened.

"Okay," she said, smiling back at Noah. "We'll go."

"Cool," Noah said, holding Keisha's gaze for a moment. "I'll see you there." He started to walk away, then turned back. "Oh—and if Jenna gives you a hard time, just tell her I invited you."

"Thanks," Keisha said, and from the look on her face, anyone passing by would have thought Noah had just given her a million dollars instead of simply inviting her to a pizza party.

"You're getting pathetic, Keish," Amanda told her when he was gone.

Keisha's smile vanished. "I am not."

"*A pizza party?*" Sam said, his hand over his heart. "*Why, I'd* love *to!*" Keisha punched him on the shoulder. "Ouch! What was that for?"

"What do you think?"

"Ah, young love," Ulf said, chuckling. "I remember when I first saw my Hildy. She was—"

"Do we have to talk about this right now?" Amanda asked. She wasn't in the mood for romantic stories—especially ones that were likely to involve goat roasts.

Both Keisha and Sam spun around and saw

her scowling at her backpack. "Is Ulf awake?" they asked. Amanda nodded.

"It's a beautiful story," the Viking grumbled.

"I'm sure it is, but right now I need to concentrate on this," Amanda said, tapping her notebook.

"No," Ulf said, holding up his substantial index finger. "Right now you need to concentrate on how you're going to launch your campaign at this peat-saw party. By the way, what *is* peat-saw? Is it meat?"

Amanda blinked a few times and stared at him. "Okay, first, it's *pizza*, Ulf, not *peat-saw*," she said. "And second, are you insane? How am I supposed to launch my campaign at Jenna's party?" It was the most ludicrous thing he'd suggested yet.

"That's a great idea!" Keisha gushed.

Amanda swung around. "Are you kidding?" she asked. "That pizza party is going to be The Jenna Scott Show. She's not going to give me any air time."

Keisha's shoulders slumped forward. "I guess you're right," she agreed.

"But maybe you don't need air time," Sam said, his eyes twinkling. "Maybe you can get by with a little *wall space*."

Amanda screwed up her face. "What are you talking about, Sam?"

"You'll see," Sam said with a mysterious smile. Then he started off down the hall.

"Where are you going?"

"To the art room—but I'll be right back. Don't leave without me, okay?"

"Okay," Amanda agreed, but she couldn't help wondering what her tall, wild-haired friend had in mind.

CHAPTER
Eight

"This is a great idea, Sam," Keisha said, finishing off the words *Littlefield for Student Council* in purple on her latest poster.

Sam had managed to get Ms. Rainey, the art teacher, to lend him a bunch of supplies from the art room—posterboard, markers, paint pens, and construction paper—and now he, Amanda, and Keisha were at Casa Napoli making posters to kick off Amanda's student council campaign.

"Thanks," Sam said. "I can't wait to see Jenna's face when she comes in here for her party tomorrow and sees all these posters for Amanda on the walls."

Instead of having Amanda's mother drop them at Quincy Market, the kids had gotten dropped off at Casa Napoli. After talking with the owner, Carmine, for a moment, they'd gotten permission to hang up as many posters as they wanted, and he had assured them that he'd keep them up through the end of next week, when the sixth-grade student council elections were taking place.

It would be great advertising for Amanda. Casa Napoli was one of the most popular pizza places in the neighborhood, and a lot of students from Adams Middle School stopped in regularly with their families and friends.

"Too bad you guys didn't get to go to the jewelry store or the CD Exchange," Amanda said.

"Or that shipping store," Ulf put in. "I would have liked to have seen their fleets. I wonder what kind of boats they had in there."

Amanda shook her head. "I already told you, Ulf. FedEx doesn't build boats. They mail packages and stuff."

"It said *shipping* on the door," Ulf insisted.

"Yeah, but it's not that kind of shipping," Amanda told him.

"And just how would you know?" the little Viking grumbled. "You admitted you've never been inside."

"Ulf!" Amanda groaned.

Sam and Keisha laughed, picking up enough of the conversation to understand what Ulf and Amanda were arguing about.

"Well, anyway, don't worry about the CD Exchange," Sam said. "I can get CDs anytime, but it's not every day that I get a chance to annoy Jenna Scott."

"You don't like her much, do you, Sam?" Keisha said with a chuckle.

"I don't like anyone who's that stuck on themselves."

"You mean like Noah Carpenter?" Amanda asked.

Keisha whirled on her. "Come on, he's not that bad," she said. "He did invite us to the pizza party."

Amanda gave her a sideways glance. "He invited *you* to the pizza party. Sam and I just happened to be nearby at the time."

"That's not true," Keisha said. "He invited all of us. Didn't he, Sam?"

"I'm not getting in the middle of this," Sam said. "But, hey—speaking of pizza." He pointed toward a waitress who was headed their way. Quickly, they gathered together all the posters and art supplies and made room on their table for the large pepperoni pizza they'd ordered.

Once the waitress had set down the silver platter and served them each a piece, Ulf stepped forward. "So *this* is pizza," he said, examining Amanda's plate.

"You want to try a little?" Amanda asked. "Or are you sticking with that 'I'll only eat it if I killed it' routine?"

Ulf jabbed at the crust with his spear. "It's just bread, isn't it?" he asked. "With cheese and—" He paused and poked the tip of his spear into a piece of pepperoni, lifting it off the pizza. "What's this?" he asked. Then, with a sneer, he said, "Chicken?"

Amanda scowled. "No," she said. "It's pepperoni."

"Pepperoni? What in Odin's name is that?"

Amanda narrowed her eyes and thought. "I'm not sure, exactly," she admitted, looking to her friends. "Um, guys? What *is* pepperoni?"

"It's some kind of meat," Keisha offered.

"It's like sausage," Sam said. "A casing stuffed with a bunch of ground-up meat."

"What's a *casing*?" Keisha asked.

"It's kind of like a sleeve made from an animal's intestine, usually a cow or sheep, I think.

They clean it out and then pack it full of ground-up meat and all kinds of spices. Then they seal up the ends and cook it," Sam answered, taking a big bite of his pizza.

"An intestine?" Amanda said, setting down her slice. "Are you sure?"

"Mm-hm," Sam mumbled through a mouthful of food.

"Gross!" Keisha exclaimed. She, too, set down her slice and began plucking off all the pepperoni. Amanda watched Keisha for a minute, and then she did the same. "If I had known that, I would have stopped eating this stuff a long time ago," Keisha said.

"Do you guys like hot dogs?" Sam asked with a mischievous grin.

Amanda shook her head. "No way, Sam. Don't even start. We're not going there."

"Why not? Don't you want to know what's in your food?"

"No!" Amanda and Keisha answered together.

Sam chuckled. "Okay, fine. But can I at least have your extra pepperoni?"

"Sure," Amanda said. She reached for the pile she'd made on her napkin, but it was gone. "Hey, where did—?"

"Delicious!" Ulf exclaimed, stuffing another piece of pepperoni into his mouth.

Amanda stared at the little Viking, aghast. He'd already eaten her entire pile of pepperoni pieces, and now he was headed for Keisha's. "I think we've found someone else who doesn't mind eating intestines," she said as a slice of pepperoni disappeared from the top of Keisha's pile.

"Hey—save some for me, Ulf!" Sam called.

"Ulf, why don't you try some of the pizza?" Amanda suggested. "There's pepperoni on every slice."

"Very well," the Viking said, walking back to Amanda. She cut off a small piece of pizza, making sure to get a little pepperoni on it, too, and offered it to him. Ulf stabbed it with his spear, then grabbed the morsel and shoved it into his mouth.

At first, Amanda didn't think he liked it. He squinted his eyes and chewed slowly, like a cow gnawing on hay. But after a moment, a wide grin lit up his face. "Pizza," he said merrily. "I like it!" Without asking, he speared another piece from Amanda's plate and devoured it, too.

"This must be the food of the gods!" he cried out when he'd finished with his second bite. He was about to spear more of Amanda's slice, but she moved her plate out of the way.

"Here—I'll get you your own piece," she told him, pulling one free from the pie. But Ulf jumped right onto the silver serving platter and began spearing and devouring pizza as if his life depended on it.

Sam, Amanda, and Keisha all watched, mesmerized by how quickly the slice on the tray was disappearing. In less than five minutes, the tiny Viking had made his way through a slice that was more than five times his size.

"Wow," Keisha said. "That's what I call a healthy appetite."

"I'll say," Sam agreed.

Amanda was about to comment, but she was interrupted by a loud burp. "Ulf!" she said. "He just belched," she explained to her friends.

"I'm not surprised," Sam said.

"Does he want . . . more?" Keisha asked.

"I think that's good for now," Ulf said. Then he stretched his arms over his head and yawned. "Pizza," he said again with a smile. "There will be more of this tomorrow, at that party, won't there?" he asked.

"Yeah, that's what people usually eat at pizza parties," Amanda said.

"Excellent!" Ulf said. And then, without further comment, he curled up at the edge of the table and went to sleep.

"What's he doing now?" Sam asked.

"Napping," Amanda said.

"He sure takes a lot of naps," Keisha commented.

"Yeah, well, at least he's not spearing anything at the moment," Amanda said, thinking of her wall at home. She still hadn't figured out how to explain that one to her mother. "So, anyway, how many more posters do you think we should do?"

Keisha thumbed through the ones they had sitting on the side of the table. "We could probably use another three," she said. "But you know what would be really cool?"

"What?"

"If we could come up with some kind of campaign slogan for you."

"Yeah, that would be cool," Amanda said. "But what should it say?"

"Maybe it should have something to do with your ideas," Sam said, nodding toward Amanda's notebook, which was lying on the chair next to her.

Amanda gazed at her notebook mournfully.

"I just wish I could figure out how to make it work," she said.

"Why don't you tell us about it," Keisha suggested. "Maybe we can help."

"All right," Amanda said. "It's this: I was hoping there was some way that I could get the middle school schedule changed so that we could have a longer lunch and some kind of recess built into the day."

"Wow," Keisha said. "That would be awesome."

"Yeah, that's a great idea," Sam agreed. "If you could do that, *everyone* would vote for you."

"Do you think so?" Amanda asked.

"Definitely," Sam said. "Lunch is way too short."

"Yeah, and I hate that we don't get recess anymore," Keisha added. "Not that I need to go out and play on the swings or anything, but it would be nice to have a break in the day, you know? Some time to say hi to friends other than just when you're passing them in the hall."

Amanda's mouth dropped open. "That's it!" she said. "Why didn't I think of it before?"

"Think of what?" Keisha asked.

"*Passing time,*" Amanda said. "It's so obvious."

She pushed her pizza aside, grabbed her notebook, and began scribbling again. *If we could just make this three minutes instead of six*, she muttered to herself, scratching away with her pencil.

"What are you doing?" Keisha and Sam asked.

"Just a second," Amanda replied, not taking her eyes—or her pencil—off her paper. "Then that gives me . . . twenty-seven minutes to work with. It's perfect!" she exclaimed, looking up at her friends. "It works!"

"What works?" Sam asked.

"My idea," Amanda said. "See, when Keisha mentioned saying hi to people when you pass them in the hall, it made me realize just how much time we have between classes. Kids are always hanging around outside classes waiting for the bell to ring!"

"So?"

"*So-o*, that means we don't need six minutes between every class to get from one room to the next, do we?" Amanda asked. "I mean, it's just a waste of time, isn't it?"

"I guess so," Keisha said.

"But if we shorten the time we have between

classes—from six minutes to, say, three—we could free up twenty-seven minutes in the day."

"Twenty-seven minutes?" Sam echoed.

"Yeah," Amanda said excitedly. "And that means that we could add a fifteen-minute break in the morning *and* have an extra twelve minutes for lunch. Wouldn't that be awesome?"

"That would be excellent," Sam said.

"And I wouldn't have to shorten any classes to do it," Amanda said. "So the teachers might even go for it."

"This is great," Keisha said. "I'm putting it on your poster. *A vote for Littlefield is a vote for longer lunches*," she said, writing as she spoke. "And on this one I'm writing, *Give yourself a break! Vote Littlefield.*"

"Clever, Keish," Sam said, copying the phrases onto two of his posters.

Amanda smiled. The slogans did have a nice ring to them. And for the first time since she'd entered the student council race, victory seemed within reach.

CHAPTER
Nine

"This is insane," Amanda said, taking in all of the decorations Jenna and her parents had managed to put up at Casa Napoli the next afternoon. There were VOTE FOR JENNA balloons, JENNA FOR STUDENT COUNCIL streamers, and even JENNA SCOTT = YOUR REPRESENTATIVE T-shirts being worn by Jenna, Emily, and Sarah.

"Do you think anyone's going to notice *our* posters?" Amanda asked Sam.

"I don't know. You think anyone's going to notice your pizza disappearing all by itself?" Sam asked.

Amanda glanced down at her plate. Sure enough, Ulf was doing his thing—spearing and eating pizza as if he were competing for a gold medal. "Ulf!" Amanda hissed.

The Viking stopped mid-spear and gazed up at her. "Whath the plobem?" he asked, his mouth packed full.

"The problem is we're in a room full of people and my pizza looks like it's part of a magic act."

"I'm hungry," Ulf protested.

"What else is new?" Amanda muttered. She gazed up at Sam with tired eyes. "I'm going to go stand in a dark corner until the bottomless pit here is done eating, okay?" But before she could get away, Michelle Burton grabbed her by the elbow.

"Great posters, Amanda!" she gushed. "I didn't know you were running for student council."

"Neither did I," Corey Russell said. "Can you really get us a longer lunch?"

"And a break?" Dylan Weeks asked.

Amanda glanced up at Sam in surprise.

"I guess people are noticing the posters," Sam commented.

"I guess so," Amanda agreed.

"So? Can you?" Corey asked. "Because I'll definitely vote for you if it means more time to eat."

Amanda looked around and blinked. While Michelle, Corey, and Dylan had been questioning her, five or six other students had crowded around, too, and now they were all waiting for her answer.

"Delicious!" Ulf called out, getting ready to spear another piece of pizza. Carefully, Amanda turned so as to hide her plate. Covertly, she handed it off to Sam.

"I'll just be over here," Sam said. "In a dark corner."

"Thanks," Amanda mouthed to him. Then she turned back to her questioners. "Actually, yeah, I think I can get us a longer lunch. And a break in the morning, too."

"But how?" someone asked.

"Yeah, how are you going to convince the teachers to give us more time to eat?" Corey asked. "They're not going to let you shorten classes or anything."

"That's the thing," Amanda said. "We wouldn't need to shorten classes. I've been looking at the schedule and I found twenty-seven minutes that we can use to make lunch a little longer and add a fifteen-minute break to the morning."

"No way!"

"That would be awesome!"

"I'm voting for Amanda," Michelle said.

"Me, too," someone else agreed. "Free pizza is cool, but I'd rather have ten more minutes for lunch every day."

As the crowd around her broke up, Amanda stared, mesmerized. It was working! People were actually planning to vote for her! Sure, they were eating Jenna's pizza, but when election time came, it looked like Amanda might get their votes.

"Nice work," Sam said, returning to her side.

"Where's Sir Eat-a-lot?" Amanda asked.

Sam placed his palms together beside his head and closed his eyes. "Sleeping like a baby," he said. "I know because he pulled a napkin over himself as a blanket."

"Sleeping," Amanda said. "Of course." She was beginning to wonder if the little Viking ever did anything but eat and sleep. "So, did you hear any of that?" she asked Sam. "People really seem to like my ideas. I think I'm actually going to get a few votes."

"I'd say you'll probably get a lot," Sam said. "Especially after you explain your idea to the whole class. When are campaign speeches, anyway?"

"Tomorrow morning," Amanda said. "And then we vote."

"Have you written yours yet?"

"Pretty much. I have to go home and tweak it tonight, though."

"I haven't even started mine," someone said. Amanda turned, surprised to see Noah Carpenter standing next to her.

"Your campaign speech?" she asked.

"Yeah," Noah said with a grin, "but that's okay. I'll probably just wing it, anyway. That's how I usually do oral book reports and stuff."

Amanda narrowed her eyes. She wasn't impressed. If anything, she was suspicious. What was Noah Carpenter doing hanging around making small talk with her and Sam? He'd never so much as looked at either one of them before unless Keisha was around.

"So, is it true that you're promising longer lunches?" he asked. "How's that work?"

So that's what he wants, Amanda thought, feeling a bit smug. Apparently, even popular people were concerned with issues when it came down to food and free time. "I've got it all figured out," Amanda said. "But you'll have to wait for my speech tomorrow to hear how." She glanced toward the front of the room where Jenna, Emily, and Sarah were handing out balloons. "I'm not about to let anyone steal my idea."

Noah blew a puff of air toward his forehead, making one of his dark curls flutter. "I don't want to steal your idea," he said. "I was just wondering if you could really do it or if you were just saying it to get elected."

Amanda clicked her tongue. "As if I'd make something up to get elected," she said. "That would be dishonest."

Noah lowered one eyebrow. "So?"

"So, that would be wrong," Amanda said. "Geez."

Noah narrowed both of his eyes and studied her face for a moment, then chuckled. "Wow, you're serious, aren't you?" he asked.

"Of course I'm serious," Amanda said.

Noah shook his head. "Huh. I didn't know anyone really cared about the student council," he said. "I thought people just wanted to be on it so they could get out of class once in a while for the meetings."

"That's not why people run for student council!" Amanda told him.

Noah shrugged. "That's why I'm running," he said. "To get out of language arts ten minutes early every Thursday."

Amanda's mouth dropped open.

Sam sucked in his breath. "Bad move," he told Noah, shaking his head.

"That's horrible!" Amanda snapped. "I can't believe anyone could be so self-centered! Student council is about making positive changes for the school—not getting out of class early! How can you even—"

"What's going on?" Keisha asked. She looked from Amanda to Sam to Noah and back again.

"Where have you been?" Sam asked.

Keisha nodded toward the back of the room. "Eating pizza and talking with people about Amanda's ideas."

"You didn't tell anyone how I'm planning to make it work, did you?" Amanda asked. "Because there are people around here who would steal my idea in a second just to get out of language arts class!" she hissed, glaring at Noah.

Noah gave Keisha a cautious stare. "Your friend is a little intense," he said, backing away. "I'll talk to you later."

Keisha watched him go, then turned to Amanda, her eyebrows knit in a puzzled frown. "What was that about?" she asked.

Amanda shook her head. "He's unbelievable."

"Something tells me you don't mean that in a good way," Keisha said.

"Noah made the mistake of telling Amanda that the reason he's running for student council is so he can get out of class early once in a while," Sam said.

Keisha clapped a hand over her mouth and giggled.

"What? You think that's funny?" Amanda demanded.

Keisha shrugged. "Maybe just a little," she said.

Amanda exhaled heavily. "I can't believe you," she said. "That boy could kick a puppy and you'd think it was sweet."

This time both Sam and Keisha laughed.

"What?" Amanda snapped.

"Don't you think you're going a little over-board?" Sam asked.

Amanda squinted at her friends. "Look. I just don't want to lose to someone who doesn't even take the student council seriously. Especially not to *him*," she added, glowering in Noah's direction.

"You should cut Noah some slack," Keisha said. "Before, when I was standing near Jenna Central, I heard him telling her that he invited the rest of the student council candidates because she said it was a party for everyone. I think she was complaining because you, Jesse, and Tracy are all here, too."

"Hmph," Amanda grunted. "I still think it's lame that he's running just to get out of class."

"Maybe," Keisha said. "But that doesn't mean that he wouldn't have good ideas if he got elected."

"Whose side are you on?" Amanda asked.

"Yours," Keisha said. "I'm voting for you. I'm just saying that Noah's not that bad. You shouldn't be so hard on him."

"Whatever," Amanda replied. She'd had about enough of the Noah Carpenter defense.

She was ready to head home. Especially when she looked up and saw Jenna and her two clones heading their way. "Oh, great," she murmured. "This should be fun." She nodded toward Jenna, Emily, and Sarah. When Sam and Keisha saw the Jenna squad approaching, they groaned, too.

"You guys aren't supposed to be here," Jenna said, cutting right to the chase.

"Nice to see you, too, Jenna," Amanda replied. "Emily, Sarah," she added, nodding at Jenna's faithful followers. "Nice shirts. Was there a sale in Jenna's closet?"

"Very funny," Jenna said, without giving Emily or Sarah a chance to respond. "Now would you like to explain what you're doing here?"

"Having some free pizza?" Sam suggested.

Jenna glared up at him. "You're not even in the sixth grade," she said. "And you two weren't invited," she added, eyeing Keisha and Amanda.

"Actually, Noah invited us," Keisha said. "He said it was for the whole sixth grade."

"Well, Noah was wrong," Jenna replied. "This is a party for people who are planning to vote for me for student council."

"Then why did you invite Noah?" Sam asked. "He's running against you."

Jenna's mouth curved into a slight grin, and she looked straight at Keisha as she answered. "I invited Noah because he's helping me," she said. "He doesn't really care about the student council, so he's telling all his friends to vote for me."

"He is not!" Keisha said.

Jenna smiled smugly and shrugged her shoulders. "You can believe what you want," she said. "But it's true. Noah!" she called, walking over to where he was standing. Amanda, Keisha, and Sam watched as she put her arm around his shoulder and whispered something to him. Noah glanced at Amanda briefly, then turned back to Jenna and laughed.

"I can't believe he would actually vote for her—or tell anyone else to," Keisha said.

"Face it, Keish," Amanda said. "Your Prince Charming is one of the gingerbread people, and the gingerbread people stick together."

"But Noah wouldn't—"

"He would, and he is," Amanda said. Then she turned to Sam. "Come on. Let's wake up the Viking. I have to go home and work on my speech. It's going to have to be really good if I want to have a shot at beating Mr. and Ms. Thing over there."

CHAPTER
Ten

The next morning before school, Amanda stood with her face buried in her locker, reading and rereading her campaign speech. She'd worked on it all night, changing words here and there to try to make it sound perfect. As far as she could tell, it had come out pretty good. But still, just knowing that Jenna could be getting a whole bunch of votes from Noah and his buddies made her wonder why she'd bothered.

"Hey, Amanda—good luck!" Michelle said as she walked by.

"Thanks," Amanda said without taking her head out of her locker. The way her voice echoed around the small metallic box, it sounded like she was speaking into a microphone.

"Keep it down!" Ulf yelled from the top shelf. Amanda had spread out a bandanna up there as a makeshift bed for the little Viking. "Some of us are trying to get a little rest."

"Do you take this many naps in your world?" Amanda asked him.

"Can't," Ulf said, shaking his head so that his red hair swished back and forth. "There's no rest for warriors. Or for explorers on the high seas. There's no pizza, either," he added. "Still, I miss it. The salty air, the adventure, new lands on the horizon."

"Yeah, we'll have to get you back there sooner or later," Amanda said.

Ulf nodded. "Maybe I'll go back after we celebrate your victory."

Amanda clunked her head into the side of her locker. "Or my defeat," she said.

"Nonsense!" Ulf called out. He stood up on the shelf and gazed down at her. "You're not going to lose. You know what your people want and you're ready to give it to them. They'll follow you across the ocean if you ask them to!"

"I think I'll settle for their votes," Amanda said. She held her palm up beside the Viking. "Come on. Let's go," she said, encouraging him to hop on.

"We can't go yet," Ulf objected. "We have to prepare for battle."

"Excuse me?" Amanda said.

"You're about to go into battle," the little Viking said, "so let's hear your battle cry!"

"My . . . what?"

"Your battle cry," the Viking repeated. "Every good warrior needs a battle cry to boost his morale before he begins a fight."

"But I'm not fighting," Amanda said.

"Of course you are," Ulf said. "You're fighting for your seat on the high council!"

"The student council."

"Same thing," Ulf said. "Now raise your right fist and repeat after me: Ballyhooooooo!" he yelled, thrusting his spear into the air.

Amanda blinked a few times and stared at the Viking. She'd always thought he was a little bit insane, but now she knew it. "I can't do that," she whispered, glancing left and right down the packed hallway. "People will think I'm crazy."

Ulf frowned, but he seemed to understand. "How about just a little yell," he suggested. "Ballyhoooooo," he repeated in a whisper.

Amanda rolled her eyes. "All right," she said, aware that Ulf wasn't going to let it go until she complied. "Ballyhooooooo," she murmured into her locker.

"Bally what?" Keisha asked.

Amanda jumped, banging her forehead against the shelf where Ulf was standing. The Viking tumbled off the shelf and landed on Amanda's shoulder, grabbing on to a stray hair at the back of her neck for balance.

"Ouch!" Amanda squealed. She snatched Ulf from her shoulder and put him back on the shelf. "So much for my battle cry," she said.

"Is that what that was?" Keisha asked. "I thought you were sneezing. How'd your speech come out?"

"It's okay," Amanda said. "But I'm pretty nervous."

"You shouldn't be," Keisha told her. "Your ideas are great. As soon as everyone hears about them, you'll be a shoo-in."

"I hope so," Amanda said. "I really want this position. Not like some *other people* I know," she added, scowling at Noah Carpenter, who was approaching.

"Hey, Keisha," Noah said. Then as an afterthought, he glanced at Amanda. "Hey," he said, but he kept his distance. Amanda crossed her arms and stared at Noah. She had nothing to say to him. But what surprised her was that it didn't look like Keisha did, either.

"I have to go," Keisha said, and gave him a disgusted look. "I'll see you in homeroom, Amanda."

As she walked off down the hall, Noah stared after her, baffled. "What's her problem?" he asked Amanda.

"You," Amanda replied.

"Me? What did I do?"

"Oh, I don't know," Amanda said sarcastically. "Maybe it's the fact that you're voting for Jenna Scott for student council and getting all your friends to vote for her, too."

Noah curled his lip. "I'm not voting for Jenna," he said.

"That's not what Jenna says."

"Well, then, Jenna's lying," Noah told her. "Because I never said I was going to vote for her. I already told you—I'm voting for myself."

"Either way, it's a wasted vote," Amanda said.

"Hey, just because I want to get out of class once in a while doesn't mean I wouldn't be a good student council—"

"Save it for your speech," Amanda said. "Oh! And don't forget to tell everyone why you're really running. That's bound to get you a bunch of votes, too."

She grabbed her books and Ulf from her locker and slammed the door. "You know, Keisha kept trying to convince me that you were okay," she told Noah. "But it looks like she's finally figured out that you're just a big two-faced fraud."

Before Noah had a chance to respond, Amanda took off down the hall, headed for homeroom. "Don't you think you were a little hard on that lad?" Ulf suggested. "He could have been telling the truth."

"Oh, please," Amanda said. "He's a big fat liar."

"But why would he tell his friends to vote for that girl when he's running for the high council, too?" Ulf asked.

"How should I know?" Amanda said. "But I don't trust him for one minute. And I'm glad Keisha finally figured out what a phony he is, too."

"I don't know," Ulf was standing on Amanda's shoulder, gazing back toward Noah. "The lad looks quite upset. He might prove to be honorable yet."

"Yeah, well, I won't hold my breath," Amanda said.

" . . . and I've had perfect attendance for five years now, so you know that I'll never miss a meeting," Jesse Hunter said, concluding his speech for the student council election.

There was a smattering of applause as Jesse stepped away from the podium that Mr. Hupp had set up to face the audience of approximately one hundred sixth graders.

"Thank you, Jesse," Mr. Hupp said. "Up next, we have Jenna Scott."

As Jenna walked to the front of the room, everyone clapped, and the applause was much louder for her introduction than it had been for either Jesse's or Tracy's speech conclusions. Of course, considering how popular she was, this was no surprise.

"Hi, everyone," Jenna said, taking her place at the podium.

"She doesn't even have note cards," Amanda whispered to Keisha out of the side of her mouth.

"Maybe she'll forget what she has to say." Keisha smiled hopefully at Amanda, and Amanda smiled back, but something told her that wasn't going to happen. Things didn't usually go badly for Jenna Scott.

"Listen up, everyone!" Ms. Garcia said, bringing the class to order. "Okay. Go ahead, Jenna."

"Thanks." Jenna looked out at her audience and smiled. *She probably just got then half their votes with that,* Amanda thought. "I want to say that I'm really excited about having a chance to be on the student council," Jenna said. "And I want everyone to know that I will work hard, and attend all the meetings, and do my best to make sure that the sixth grade is well represented."

Emily and Sarah started to clap, but they were silenced by Mrs. MacKnight. "Let's wait until she's finished," the teacher said.

Jenna went on. "I'll work hard as your student council representative, and one of the things I'm going to try to do is get us more dances and fun activities. So I hope you'll all vote for me. I promise you won't regret it."

As Jenna stepped down from the podium, loud applause filled the room.

"What are they clapping for?" Keisha said. "She didn't say anything good."

"She doesn't have to," Amanda said. "She's Jenna Scott."

"And you're Amanda Littlefield!" Ulf boomed, raising his spear over his head. "Ballyhoooooo!"

Amanda gazed down at the Viking and sighed. She was glad nobody else could hear him.

"Thank you, Jenna," Mr. Hupp said when the applause had died down. "We have only two more candidates to hear from—Amanda Littlefield and Noah Carpenter." At the mention of Noah's name, several of the boys in the room began clapping and hollering, but they were silenced by all the teachers.

"All right, Amanda, you're up," said Mr. Hupp.

As Amanda walked to the front of the room, she couldn't help feeling she'd left her stomach behind—as if she had an empty cavern below her ribs that was teeming with butterflies.

"Think might! Think strength!" a voice said in her ear, and all at once Amanda realized that Ulf had come along for the ride. She'd intended to leave him at her seat. "This is your battle to fight, and your battle to win!" Ulf went on as Amanda stepped past her classmates. "You are invincible! You are unconquerable! You have the grace of Freyja and the power of Odin behind you! Ballyhoooooooo!" the Viking yelled out, but the end of his battle cry was muffled when Amanda shoved him under the podium.

By the time Amanda had collected herself and was ready to speak, any applause there might have been had died down. Amanda had been so nervous during her walk to the front— and Ulf had been so loud—that she wasn't sure anyone had clapped at all. Of course, Keisha probably had, and maybe Michelle and Corey, too. They were both watching her with excited smiles at the moment, so it stood to reason that they would have applauded for her. In fact, Amanda was sure they must have. Corey would applaud anyone who was going to get him a longer lunch.

Amanda glanced down at her note cards and saw that her hands were shaking.

"What are you waiting for?" Ulf shouted from under the podium. "Give the mongrels what they want! And keep it short—no one likes a windbag."

Amanda chuckled slightly at the Viking's last comment, bringing her hand to her mouth and coughing to cover her amusement. "Hi, everyone," she said, trying to smile as winningly as Jenna, but somehow she didn't seem to have the same effect. *Better just get to the point,* she told herself.

"Like everyone else, I plan to work hard and attend all the student council meetings. I'd also like to help plan lots of fun activities for our class and our school. But one thing I'd really like to do as your student council representative is to help make school both a fun and productive place for us to be all the time."

Amanda paused to look up from her first note card. Her father, who taught English at the high school, had convinced her to add the word *productive* for the benefit of her teachers, and it looked as if it had been a good move. Both Mr. Hupp and Mrs. MacKnight were nodding thoughtfully. Unfortunately, the teachers weren't the ones voting.

"Cut to the chase!" Ulf called out. He was in the process of climbing onto the podium. "Don't bore them to death!"

Amanda grabbed the little Viking and stuffed him into the desk that the podium was resting on. "I can't help you from in here!" he cried.

Exactly, Amanda thought. She flipped to her

second note card and continued. "One way I think I can help make the school day better is by rearranging the schedule so that we can have a longer lunch and a mid-morning break." At that, several students in the room began to applaud, but the teachers quieted them down. "And I've come up with a way to do this that I think will work for students *and* teachers."

This time when Amanda looked up from her note cards, she saw that she had the attention of everyone in the room. "See—right now, we have six minutes between every class, which doesn't sound like a lot, I know, but really is. I checked around, and at Lincoln Middle School, students only have four minutes to get to their classes. At both Washington and Monroe, students only have three minutes between classes, and both of those schools are much bigger than ours. So, I thought that if we cut our passing time down to three minutes, too, we could use the extra time to do two things.

"First, we could have a fifteen-minute break between period two and period three. That would help to break up the morning and give students a chance to visit so that they don't have to use class time to socialize. Second, we could take the remaining twelve minutes and add that on to lunchtime. I've heard a lot of students complain that they don't have enough time to eat, and lots of times people are late to period six because they're trying to finish their lunches."

Amanda glanced up to see lots of students nodding and whispering excitedly. Even the teachers seemed to be considering what she was saying. A rush of adrenaline surged through Amanda's body. "Ballyhoooooooooo!" Ulf cried from inside the desk, and for a split second, Amanda considered joining him. But she thought better of it and decided to finish her speech instead.

"So, as you can see," she concluded, "adding a break in the morning and some more time on to lunch could help both students and teachers. If you elect me to the student council, I'll work hard to change our schedule. But I won't stop there. This is just one of my ideas. I'd also like to create a student lounge in the school—with couches and chairs and tables—where students can hang out during study halls." There were several oohs and ahhs from her classmates, so

Amanda knew that people were interested in this idea, too. But she also knew that Ulf was right—nobody liked a windbag, so she needed to wrap it up. "Overall, I just want you to know that if you elect me as your student council representative, I'll work hard to improve our school, and I'll keep fighting for you all year long. I hope you'll all consider voting for me. Thank you."

As Amanda gathered together her note cards and stepped away from the podium, the room went wild. People were applauding louder for her than they had for anyone else—including Jenna Scott!

"That was great, Amanda!" Keisha said when she returned to her seat. "You're going to win!"

"Do you really think so?"

Keisha nodded enthusiastically, and for a moment Amanda dared to believe her.

"Thank you, Amanda," Mr. Hupp said. "Now we have one more candidate to hear from—Noah Carpenter."

Noah stood up and started toward the podium, and once again applause filled the room. But this time, people weren't just clapping politely, as they had when everyone else was introduced. The applause for Noah's introduction nearly matched the applause that Amanda had gotten after presenting her whole speech.

"I'm sunk," Amanda said. Noah Carpenter was just as popular as Jenna Scott—maybe even more popular. And whether he told his friends to vote for Jenna or just kept all their votes for himself didn't really matter. Either way, he was sure to draw a big chunk of votes away from Amanda.

"Hey," Noah said when he got up to the podium. He gave everyone his quirky sideways smile, then looked straight at Keisha and added a special one just for her.

Amanda watched as Keisha crossed her arms and looked away. *Good,* she thought. *At least she's not buying his act anymore.*

"Uh . . . I just want to say that I've decided not to run for student council," Noah said. There were gasps all over the room, and Keisha's head whipped back around.

"What's he doing?" she mouthed to Amanda, but Amanda just shrugged. She was as surprised as Keisha.

"I don't think I'm going to have time for it with basketball coming up and all," Noah went on, "but I did want to say that anyone who was planning to vote for me should vote for Amanda Littlefield, instead. She's going to get us a longer lunch!" he added, thrusting his fist into the air. "That's all—thanks," Noah said, stepping down. As he walked back to his seat, everyone in the room started cheering.

Amanda sat staring at the front of the room. Had she heard right? Had Noah Carpenter actually just told everyone to vote for her? She turned toward Keisha and knew immediately from the grin on her friend's face that that was exactly what he had done.

"What do you think of him now?" Keisha asked, her smile stretching all the way across her face.

"I told you the lad had honor," Ulf said.

Amanda looked down at the Viking and then back at Keisha and swallowed hard. "All right," she said reluctantly. "So maybe he's not *all* bad."

CHAPTER
Eleven

"I still can't believe I won!" Amanda said, helping herself to an extra-big scoop of chocolate chip cookie dough ice cream. In honor of her victory, Amanda's mother had encouraged her to invite Sam and Keisha over for a mini ice-cream party, and she'd stopped and picked up a variety of flavors on the way home.

"I'm not surprised," Mr. Littlefield said. He'd taken a break from grading papers to join them. He glanced at Keisha and Sam. "Amanda's always had a great sense of justice. She'll be a wonderful student council rep."

"Thanks, Dad," Amanda said. "By the way, I think your suggestions helped a lot. My speech went really well."

"No," Keisha said. "It was amazing! I wish you could have heard it, Sam."

"Yeah," Sam said, digging into his combination of moose tracks and mint chocolate chip. "I tried to get out of band, but Mr. Snow wouldn't give me a pass."

"Too bad," Keisha said, taking a bite of black raspberry. "You would have loved it. She totally blew Jenna Scott out of the water. No one was even considering voting for her by the time Amanda was done."

"I'm not surprised," Sam said, turning to Amanda. "I've never seen you lose a fight once you put your mind to it."

"It wasn't a fight. It was an election," Amanda said. "You're starting to sound like Ulf."

"Ulf?" Mr. Littlefield asked as he scraped the last bits of ice cream from his bowl.

"Uh . . . just this funny kid at school," Amanda said.

"Who's always talking about battles and stuff," Sam added.

"Oh," Mr. Littlefield said, nodding with understanding. He got up to rinse his bowl in the sink and then put it in the dishwasher.

"Well, thanks for the ice-cream party," he said, "and congratulations again, Amanda. I'm proud of you."

"Thanks, Dad," Amanda said.

"Gotta get back to work!" Mr. Littlefield said with a wave.

"See you later, Mr. Littlefield," Sam said as Amanda's father left the kitchen. Once he was gone, Sam turned to Amanda. "Hey, speaking of the little guy—"

"Where is he?" Keisha asked.

Amanda set down her spoon. "You're going to love this," she said. "Follow me." Keisha and Sam followed Amanda into the bathroom just off the kitchen. "Take a look," Amanda told her friends as she opened the door.

There, in a bathtub full of water, was a toy Viking ship complete with red-and-white sails and three pairs of oars.

"Is he on there?" Keisha asked.

"I said stroke, you lazybones!" Ulf called to six plastic men who were seated in rowing positions.

"Oh, yeah, he's on there," Amanda said. "And it's about time he found a bathtub," she added in a whisper. Keisha and Sam laughed.

"It's my little brother's boat. He was playing with it during his bath last night and I thought Ulf should have a turn."

"It's nice to be back on the water," the Viking called out, "but I could do with a decent crew."

Amanda repeated his comment to her friends and Sam laughed. "Yeah, I bet it's hard to get a good day's work out of those guys," he said.

"I've never seen a lazier bunch of good-for-nothings in my life," Ulf agreed with a hearty chuckle.

Keisha turned to Amanda then with a serious look. "You know, now that he's helped you out and everything, we should probably get him back into the book."

"Funny she should mention that. I was thinking the same thing myself," Ulf called out from the deck of his plastic boat.

"Really?" Amanda asked.

"Oh, yes," Ulf said. "Don't get me wrong, this ship is nice and all, but I think it's probably time I went back to my world—back to my family and my crew. Back to my adventures."

Amanda pressed her lips together. "About that," she said. She'd been dreading this moment for over a week now. She gazed at her friends tentatively. "I'm not so sure that we *can* put him back."

Both Sam and Keisha narrowed their eyes. "What do you mean?" Keisha asked. "Of course we can. We just touch the page with the bracelet and *bam!*—back he goes."

Amanda wrung her hands and gazed nervously at her friends. "Well, I didn't really want to mention this but . . . "

"But what?" Sam asked, his arms folded across his chest.

"Well, I tried to put Ulf back in the book right after we got him out, but it didn't work."

"You did what?" Sam said.

"I tried to put him back," Amanda said. "That night after I brought him home. I didn't think he was going to be any help, so after he fell asleep, I tried to put him back and get the goddess instead, but it didn't work. Sorry, Ulf," she added, shooting the Viking a guilty glance.

To Amanda's surprise, Ulf just laughed. "I said you were a fiery one, too!" he boomed.

"Maybe you did something wrong," Keisha suggested.

Amanda shook her head. "I don't think so," she said. "I touched the page with the bracelet and I set Ulf right on top of his ship, but nothing happened."

"Maybe it's because he was asleep," Keisha suggested.

"Or maybe you can't put someone back in right after you get them out," Sam offered.

"Maybe," Amanda said.

"Or maybe Ulf has to be ready to jump back in himself," Keisha added.

"It could be any of those things," Sam said.

"Or a million others," Keisha said. "But there's only one way to find out."

Amanda gulped. She knew her friends were right—she had to try again. The problem was, she was nervous about it. Partly because she was worried that it wouldn't work, and partly because she was worried that it would. As much as Ulf's eating habits, table manners, and battle cries had irritated her, she was actually going to miss the little guy.

"Well, what do you say, Ulf? Are you ready to

go back?" She lowered her hand next to the Viking ship, and Ulf stepped on.

"I believe I am," he said. "I've enjoyed this world of yours, but it's time for me to get back to mine."

"Yeah, I guess it is," Amanda said. She turned to her friends. "Okay. Let's make it happen."

Keisha and Sam followed Amanda to her room, where the book was lying open on her desk. Sam flipped to Ulf's story, stopping on the page with the picture of Viking ships on the sea and Freyja in the clouds.

"Are you sure you're ready, Ulf?" Amanda asked as she prepared to use the bracelet.

The little Viking held up his hand. "Actually," he said, "there is one thing I'd like to take care of first." He untied his cape and, in a sweeping motion, flipped it off his back and set it on the floor in front of him. To Amanda's surprise, underneath the cape, he was wearing a crude knapsack. He took this off, too, placed it on the ground, and opened up the top of it. Then he reached in and pulled out a small, deep-blue crystal, which he handed to Amanda.

"What's this?" Amanda asked, taking the bean-size gem in her hand.

"Water sapphire," Ulf told her. "It's a crystal my people have mined for years. We use it for navigation in our travels by looking through it to determine the position of the sun on the horizon."

"Wow, it's beautiful," Amanda said, turning the crystal over in her hands.

"That *is* beautiful," Keisha agreed.

"Wait—you can see it?" Amanda asked.

Keisha blinked a few times and nodded. She was obviously as shocked as Amanda.

"Hey, I can, too," Sam said. "And I know what it is. That's iolite. The Vikings used it as a navigational tool."

"That's what Ulf just said," Amanda told him. "Only he called it water sapphire."

"Either way, it's gorgeous," Keisha said.

"I'm glad you all like it," the Viking said. "I want you to keep it so you'll always remember that Ulf the Red was here."

"I don't think I could ever forget that," Amanda said. "But won't you need it when you get back to your ship?"

"I have plenty of other crystals on board," Ulf said. "This one is for you."

"Thanks, Ulf," Amanda said. Then she

began looking around her room. "Shoot. I wish I had something to give you."

"You've given me plenty," the little Viking said. "I've enjoyed my adventures here, and when I get back to my world, I will tell my people about . . . *pizza*," he said, pronouncing the word as though it had mystical qualities.

Amanda laughed. "Okay," she said. "You do that. I hope they like it as much as you do."

Ulf refastened his cape around his neck and glanced down at the book. "Shall we?"

Amanda nodded. "Here goes nothing," she said, glancing up at her friends. But this time, when she touched the bracelet to the picture, everything happened just the way it was supposed to. The illustration began to swirl so that the watercolor ocean looked like a puddle of blue.

"Good luck finding new worlds!" Amanda said as the Viking gazed up at her.

"Good luck leading your council!" he called back as he jumped onto the page. All at once there was a blinding flash, and when the spots had disappeared from in front of Amanda's eyes, the little Viking was gone.

"Look! There he is!" Sam cried, pointing at the picture of the ship.

Keisha and Amanda crowded around the book and peered down at the Viking. "So that's what he looked like," Keisha said.

"Yep, that's him," Amanda agreed.

"He's kind of cute," Keisha said. Both Amanda and Sam grimaced at her. "In a rough sort of way," she added.

"Just be glad you never had to watch him eat," Amanda said, and all three of them laughed.

Get Ready for Charm Club
Book #7:
love stone

"How was the meeting?" Sam asked as Amanda walked out of the music room, having met with the student council for the first time since being elected.

"It was awesome," Amanda said. "We talked a lot about changing the schedule, and everyone really seems to be behind it. Even Mr. March thinks it could work. He's talking about phasing it in at the end of this quarter."

"That's great, Amanda," Keisha said. "And to think you owe it all to Noah Carpenter."

"I don't owe it all to him," Amanda said. "It was my idea that got me elected."

"Hey, let's not forget about Ulf," Sam said. "That little Viking was a huge help, and you can thank me for that."

"You?"

"Sure—you thought he'd be useless," Sam said. "I'm the one who convinced you that a Viking warrior was exactly what you needed."

"You can think whatever you want, Sam Sullivan," Amanda said. "But if you ask me, that little Viking was more trouble than he was worth."

"How can you say that after everything he did for you?" Sam asked.

"He did give you that cool crystal," Keisha reminded her.

"I know," Amanda said. "Ulf *was* fun to have around—even though he was a little uncivilized. And you're right, Keish, the water sapphire is really pretty. I finally figured out how to attach it to the charm bracelet. Want to see?"

"Sure," Sam and Keisha said together.

Amanda pushed up the sleeve of her vintage satin jacket.

"What's wrong?" Keisha asked, seeing her friend's face fall.

"The bracelet!" she exclaimed, gazing up with wide eyes. "It's gone!"

Jenna Scott walked into the gym for her cheerleading meeting after school. A bunch of seventh- and eighth-grade girls were already sitting on the bleachers. There were some sixth graders there, too, but not many. Only a few of them ever made the cheerleading squad, which was mostly made up of seventh and eighth graders. Most sixth graders considered trying out to be a waste of time.

But it won't be for me, Jenna told herself as she crossed the large room. *I'm going to make it!* She had to. After losing the student council election to Amanda Littlefield, of all people, she needed to get back a little of her dignity.

Plus, being on the cheerleading squad would give her more time to hang out with Noah Carpenter—who was sure to make the basketball team. He'd been avoiding her lately. It was hard to believe, but he seemed to have developed some sort of freakish crush on Keisha Johnson. Of course, that would be over as soon as he saw Jenna in her cheerleading uniform.

Smiling at the thought, Jenna headed for the bleachers to sit down between Allison Sanchez and Kana Terauchi, two popular eighth graders who were already on the squad. But on her way there, something shiny on the floor caught her eye.

Jenna stooped down and picked up a silver

bracelet with several charms on it—an angel, a unicorn, a fairy, a princess, an interesting amber-colored bead, and a beautiful blue gemstone. It looked vaguely familiar to her, as if she'd seen someone wearing it before, but she couldn't remember who.

"I guess I should take you to the lost-and-found," she muttered to the bracelet, but when she checked her watch, she saw that it was almost time for the cheerleading meeting to start.

Oh, well, Jenna thought, stuffing the bracelet into her pocket. It would have to wait. Right now, she needed to focus so she'd know what she needed to practice for tryouts. She'd go to the school lost-and-found in the morning. Surely holding on to it overnight wouldn't be a big deal. After all, the person who'd lost it probably hadn't even noticed it was missing yet. . . .